MW00850369

The Grave Robber

Also From Darynda Jones

CHARLEY DAVIDSON SERIES

First Grave on the Right
For I have Sinned: A Charley Short Story
Second Grave on the Left
Third Grave Dead Ahead
Fourth Grave Beneath my Feet
Fifth Grave Past the Light
Sixth Grave on the Edge
Seventh Grave and No Body
Eight Grave After Dark
Brighter than the Sun: A Reyes Novella
The Dirt on Ninth Grave
The Curse of Tenth Grave
Eleventh Grave in Moonlight
The Trouble with Twelfth Grave
Summoned to Thirteenth Grave
The Graveyard Shift: A Charley Novella
The Gravedigger's Son: A Charley Novella
The Graveside Bar and Grill: A Charley Novella

BETWIXT & BETWEEN

Betwixt
Bewitched
Beguiled
Moonlight and Magic

THE NEVERNEATH

A Lovely Drop
The Monster

MYSTERY

SUNSHINE VICRAM SERIES

A Bad Day for Sunshine
A Good Day for Chardonnay
A Hard Day for a Hangover

YOUNG ADULT

DARKLIGHT SERIES

Death and the Girl Next Door
Death, Doom, and Detention
Death and the Girl He Loves

The Grave Robber

A Charley Davidson Novella

By Darynda Jones

1001 DARK NIGHTS
PRESS

The Grave Robber
A Charley Davidson Novella
By Darynda Jones

1001 Dark Nights

ISBN: 979-8-88542-023-5

Published by 1001 Dark Nights Press, an imprint of Evil Eye Concepts, Incorporated

Acknowledgments from the Author

Thank you, Dear Reader, for giving me another opportunity to play in Charley's world! Eric and Halle's story was so fun. I hope you enjoy reading it as much as I loved writing it.

A special thank you to Liz, Jillian, M.J., and everyone at 1001 Dark Nights. What an honor it is to work with you.

And thank you, Chelle, from the very bottom of my grammarly-challenged heart. You rock so hard. So, so hard.

One Thousand and One Dark Nights

Once upon a time, in the future…

I was a student fascinated with stories and learning. I studied philosophy, poetry, history, the occult, and the art and science of love and magic. I had a vast library at my father's home and collected thousands of volumes of fantastic tales.

I learned all about ancient races and bygone times. About myths and legends and dreams of all people through the millennium. And the more I read the stronger my imagination grew until I discovered that I was able to travel into the stories... to actually become part of them.

I wish I could say that I listened to my teacher and respected my gift, as I ought to have. If I had, I would not be telling you this tale now.
But I was foolhardy and confused, showing off with bravery.

One afternoon, curious about the myth of the Arabian Nights, I traveled back to ancient Persia to see for myself if it was true that every day Shahryar (Persian: شهريار, "king") married a new virgin, and then sent yesterday's wife to be beheaded. It was written and I had read that by the time he met Scheherazade, the vizier's daughter, he'd killed one thousand women.

Something went wrong with my efforts. I arrived in the midst of the story and somehow exchanged places with Scheherazade – a phenomena that had never occurred before and that still to this day, I cannot explain.

Now I am trapped in that ancient past. I have taken on Scheherazade's life and the only way I can protect myself and stay alive is to do what she did to protect herself and stay alive.

Every night the King calls for me and listens as I spin tales. And when the evening ends and dawn breaks, I stop at a point that leaves him breathless and yearning for more. And so the King spares my life for one more day, so that he might hear the rest of my dark tale.

As soon as I finish a story... I begin a new one... like the one that you, dear reader, have before you now.

Author's Note

This book contains elements of suicide that some may find disturbing.

If you or someone you know is in crisis or emotional distress, there are resources available—all day, every day.

Remember, the world is a better place with you in it.

The National Suicide Prevention Lifeline

The National Suicide Prevention Lifeline provides free and confidential emotional support.

Within the United States, just text or call: **988**

Online chat: **suicidepreventionlifeline.org**

Chapter One

My body is less like a temple
and more like a bar and grill.
—Meme

I needed to get drunk. Or laid. Fortunately, I was in the right place for either if I played my cards right. Unfortunately, I hadn't shaved in three days. Was the scruffy biker look still a thing? I had my eye on a saucy redhead, a server in the bar I'd ridden twenty hours to get to. I never dreamed I'd drive two days to drink in a bar I'd never seen, in a state I could barely find on a map, but I realized rather quickly why my high-school buddy had set up shop in northern Idaho. The lush countryside and abundance of lakes proved intoxicating. Much like the beer I currently nursed, thanks to a dispute that involved a gas pump, a broken card reader, and an irate blonde.

I shook out of my thoughts with gritted teeth and studied my friend's grunge-worthy establishment. Exposed metal rafters, corrugated walls, and neon signs were the foundation of Jason's decor. But the coolest thing about Cruisers was a road that cut through the building, created by two large garage doors at either end. It allowed bikers to ride through and show off their pride and joys while other patrons cheered them on. The tradition created a type of subculture among the local riders and enhanced the spirit of camaraderie and brotherhood—something I understood very well.

After the most recent celebration died down, the patrons applauding a vintage Indian Chief that gave the air a smoky hue as it passed through, I refocused on the guy I hadn't seen in more years than I cared to admit. Jason Vigil. Tall, slim, and athletic, with dark hair and an easy smile. The scrapper hadn't changed at all. And he'd done well—not that I was surprised. But to have the bar filled to near-capacity at four in the afternoon on a weekday attested to the popularity of the place. And its owner.

While employees hustled to get ready for the evening rush, including the redhead, another biker revved his engine, and the scent of gasoline set me on edge yet again.

"I'm not kidding," I said to Jason, veering back onto the same highway I'd been trying to exit for half an hour. "She went ballistic for no reason. How the fuck was I supposed to know she'd been waiting for that pump? And was it really worth all that?"

I tipped an icy bottle of Corona to my lips and drained the last drop as Jason fought a grin. He gestured to another of his servers, summoning a curvy brunette to our table.

"Hey, handsome," she said to me, but the constant glances she'd been throwing Jason's way for the last half hour, ones full of adoration and those little cartoon hearts, told me exactly where her interests lay. And she planned on keeping them there.

Jason frowned regardless. "This is Eric."

"I figured." She flashed me a flirtatious smile. It was hard to blame her. The girl lived off tips. And the heated glare I received from Jason as a result was well worth the C-note I'd drop on the table before leaving. "Eric Constantine Vause," she said, giving me a thorough once-over. "That's probably the coolest name in recorded history."

I couldn't have stopped the arrogant grin that took over my face if I'd tried. "I like to think so. I take it Jason told you about his slightly younger, much better-looking partner in crime?"

Jason cleared his throat a little too loudly.

She laughed and picked up the empty bottles. "I'm Betty. Two more?"

I nodded, and she took off toward the bar, swaying her hips for Jason's benefit and gifting me another chance to study a kid sitting alone on a stool. One who looked like he'd only recently given up training wheels yet was currently downing his third shot of whiskey despite that fact.

He raised his hand for another.

I shook my head, checked my watch, and went back to drawing on a napkin. Not the way I usually expressed my creativity, but desperate times and all that. "Anyway," I said, the agitation fizzling, "someone should check the water here. Chick was unstable as fuck."

Jason finally caved and let a shit-eating grin spread across his face. "She was beautiful, I take it?"

I stopped drawing and gaped at him for a solid thirty seconds before tossing my pen onto the table and leaning back in my chair. "Fuck off," I said under my breath, dangerously close to sounding like an impetuous child. She *was* beautiful. Breathtaking. But that had nothing to do with the current situation.

Jason took the beers from Betty with a nod of thanks and placed both on the table in front of me. "I'm sorry, man. I wouldn't have invited you if I'd known this would happen."

"Liar."

"No, really. This trip was supposed to be relaxing. A chance to get away from it all."

I wrapped my fingers loosely around the neck of one of the beers and took a long draw, feeling like shit for whining about something so meaningless when I should be catching up with my oldest and dearest. "It is. It will be. I just need to chill."

I honestly couldn't figure out why the incident bothered me so much. Maybe because I could already see the headline. *Video Goes Viral When Undermedicated Woman Loses Her Shit at Gas Station.*

All because I'd pulled into a nearby convenience store to top off before hooking up with Jason. The pumps were all taken, save one. I'd eased into the spot and turned off my engine, only to have a woman driving a black Chevy short bed at the next pump get out of her truck and start screaming at me. Apparently, the card reader at her pump wasn't working, and she'd been waiting for the one I'd pulled into.

No clue how I was supposed to know that.

I ignored her, filled my tank in under a minute, then straddled my Harley again before giving her my full attention.

She stood glaring at me as a soft breeze filtered sunlight through her silky blond hair. Hair that brushed her face like it craved the touch. When I continued to stare—partly in belligerence and partly in awe—she went off again, shouting at me about fucking manners and fucking motorcycles and fucking morons from New Mexico. She'd probably recorded my plate to report me to the gas pump police. So, I started my engine and revved it to drown out her curse words. I have sensitive ears.

My actions only fueled her rage. Every time she opened her mouth—the pretty one with lips like overripe peaches—I revved the engine again, not even trying to hide the smirk I wore as I adjusted the strap on my helmet with my free hand.

If not for the tears shimmering in her eyes, threatening to spill over remarkably dark lashes and slide down smooth, flushed cheeks, I wouldn't have given up the game so soon. But she was clearly disturbed, so I put the bike in gear and started to drive off.

The massive red truck behind me, waiting for the spot I was about to vacate, gave me pause. She was seconds away from losing the pump again, and despite her mental state—or maybe because of it—I didn't want to see that happen. I hooked a thumb over my shoulder, indicating the dually, then pointed an index finger, half-shrouded by a black leather glove, toward her pickup.

She caught on quickly. Her eyes widened with realization, and she hurried back to her single cab. As she eased it forward, I backed away from the pump, blocking the red truck's entrance until she'd staked a solid claim.

The bird I got from the other driver for that maneuver sat better with me than the tears I'd gotten from the woman, so I left the station baffled, agitated, and oddly satisfied.

I'd laugh about it later. Much later. For now, I prayed there wasn't an actual video. Surely, people had better things to do.

It took Jason crossing his arms over his chest and leaning back in his chair to assess me in more depth for me to snap back to the present. I glanced at the kid again, checked my watch, then questioned my friend with a gentle arch of my brow. I was sophisticated like that.

Jason's expression was both curious and cautious. He squinted and circled an index finger at me as he went through a mental checklist. "Same dark hair with the requisite bad haircut."

"Bad?" I asked, only slightly offended.

"Same shifty eyes."

"Shifty?"

"Same stubborn jaw."

I lifted one corner of my mouth. "Some would call it strong."

"Even with all of that—"

"Masculine."

"—you're different."

"Rakish, even."

"You've changed."

I picked up the beer, downed it, and set the bottle on the table before tossing the guy a reassuring smirk. "You haven't."

He scoffed. "You might be surprised."

I gestured toward Betty. "Besides the fact that you've upped your game, that is." I studied the brunette, who was several years older than Jason, and peered into a moment nobody had a right to see. Nobody in their right mind, anyway.

Sadly, I'd never been in my right mind, even as a kid. But a traumatic event five years ago made me even more of a freak, and over time I learned to do things that would challenge even the most open of minds.

And this instance was no different. I relaxed and let the moment drift into my mind. Decades from now, Betty would lay in a hospital bed, surrounded by the diverse family she'd accumulated. A ragtag collection of castoffs, children she and her husband had taken in, a surrogate aunt here, a lost-and-found grandfather there, and a small but tight-knit army of bikers, the most loyal people on Earth. And by her side, holding her fragile hand, was her husband, Jason, aged yet somehow still handsome. Fucker.

I gestured toward the brunette with a nod and looked back at said fucker. "She's a good person."

"She meets your approval?" Jason asked, surprise registering in the barely perceptible rounding of his hazel eyes. "That's a first."

It was, indeed. "Maybe you'll actually listen this time." Three failed marriages were enough for most people to swear off the age-old tradition. Not Jason Vigil. The man was nothing if not determined. "There's just one problem," I added.

Jason made a resigned hissing sound and sat back in his chair. "Here it comes."

"She's too good for you."

After a long, contemplative moment, Jason nodded. "I'm very aware." He watched me, his gaze glistening and sharp as though he were trying to see into my soul.

Good luck with that. It was as black and murky as a thunderhead at midnight. No amount of staring could penetrate that much swirling darkness.

"Someday, you're going to have to tell me how you do that," Jason said. "How you always know."

I made a half-hearted attempt at a smile. "Someday," I lied.

I'd grown up with gut feelings about people. Everyone has them, but my instincts were never wrong. So much so my friends accused me of being psychic. But after an ancient demon who wanted to take over the world possessed me five years ago, before a sassy, godlike creature from Albuquerque ripped it out of me—with the help of a Rottweiler named Artemis—my powers of intuition had multiplied tenfold. They'd morphed into an actual supernatural ability, for lack of a better phrase. A sleep-depriving, morbid, nightmarish ability. One I was still trying to come to terms with.

I glanced at the kid yet again, then at my watch, growing more anxious as the time drew near.

"You got somewhere to be?" Jason asked.

"Not yet." I took note of the kid's dirty hair and torn denim jacket, which looked three sizes too big. "What? You don't card people here?"

Jason followed my line of sight. "Zachary Church. He's a kid from the neighborhood. Looks younger than he is."

"There is no way that baby-faced punk, who's about two shots away from puking his guts out, is twenty-one."

"As of last week."

"Ah." I reached for the second bottle of Corona, but Jason swiped it from under my nose and downed half the contents before I could utter a single protest.

"What?" he asked when he paused for a breath. "You were taking too long."

Realization dawned. "You just did that so you could call that cute server over again."

"Does that surprise you?"

"Not in the least. I was thinking about asking for her number."

Jason's jaw went slack seconds before he slammed it shut so hard the muscles jumped in protest.

"You know, a test of sorts."

His hand tightened around the bottle.

"Make sure she's really into you."

His other hand curled into a fist.

I let my second-best grin, the slow and calculated one, spread across my face. "That's what you get for drinking my beer, asshole."

Jason held onto his irritation for a few gloriously tense seconds before letting the agitation drain from his body. Good thing. The guy punched like a sledgehammer. He drew in a deep breath and chose his voice over violence. "Does that mean you're actually going to pay for your drinks this time?"

"As long as I get the ninety-seven percent friends-and-family discount."

It was Jason's turn to arch a sophisticated brow. "And you think you qualify?"

That hurt. I grabbed my chest, hoping to generate some Oscar buzz, and whispered, "Ouch."

Jason scoffed and ordered two more beers while I returned to my drawing. He gave me a minute before clearing his throat.

I ignored him.

"Now that I have your undivided attention—"

He didn't.

"—I have a confession to make."

Getting closer.

"And a favor to ask."

Intrigue won out. Damn it. I put the pen down. My drawing sucked, anyway. "Don't tell me that rash came back. That was a one-time deal, buddy." I held up an index finger to drive my point home. "I smelled like menthol ointment for three days." That stuff would not wash off.

"What? No." Jason scooted closer to shush me. "My invitation wasn't one hundred percent altruistic."

I blinked at him, waiting for more info.

"I have a friend in trouble."

Dread slithered up my spine, leaving a trail of ice in its wake. Jason was the most down-to-earth guy I knew. He didn't have a manipulative bone in his body. Why would he invite me to Idaho without giving me the real reason unless he was certain I would flat-out refuse? And there was only one reason I would do that.

"Your kind of trouble."

Oh, hell no.

I was done. No more dead people. No more hellhounds trying to cuddle in the middle of the night. And no more asshole demons attempting to worm their way into my brain. That was the plan, anyway, and I was sticking to it. Through sheer force of will, I held the fact that my abilities followed me no matter how far I ran at bay. Swimming in a luxurious state of denial. And I would've stayed there if not for the kid.

I glanced at him again, wondering how many shots he could take before getting intimately acquainted with the floor. Apparently, he wondered the same thing. He downed yet another shot, coughed up his left lung, then raised his hand for another.

Thankfully, the bartender cut him off with a warning shake of his head.

"Vause," Jason said.

"Vigil," I said back.

He sighed loudly enough to be heard over the din. "Eric."

"Jason." He would run out of names soon. Then where would we be?

"I'll never understand how you do what you do."

"I'm on vacation," I lied. I wasn't on vacation. I was done. Canada was calling my name, and I had every intention of answering. Right after I saw to the kid at the bar.

"It's just…the stuff you said the other night when I called..."

I started drawing again, desperately trying to get the shading right. "I'm still on vacation."

"Can you really see that shit?"

"Yeah, but I'm on vacation." It would help if I knew what I was drawing. And if I wasn't drawing it on a napkin.

"Ghosts and demons and hellhounds?"

I stopped and put all my frustration into a single accusatory glare. "When you called, I was about six bottles too many into a really rough night. I shouldn't have said anything."

"But seriously. Hellhounds?" He looked around to make sure no one was listening before continuing, his tone conspiracy-theory soft. "Like, they're a real thing?"

"They're really quite sweet once you get to know them."

"And the grim reaper is real? 'Cause I'm not gonna lie, I haven't been able to sleep since you told me."

"Right? And you haven't even met her."

He reared back in his chair as if I'd told him the world was about to end. Or that he had a hair out of place. "Her?"

"She's a peach. No, wait." I squinted in thought, then amended my statement. "She's like a deadly peach. Like a peach with a claymore inside."

Jason chose that moment to get offended. "All this time, dude. All these years, and you never told me what was going on."

I decided to give him something to actually be offended about. "You were busy getting married. And then divorced. And then re-married. And then divorced. And then—"

"I get it," he said, his tone razor-wire sharp. "Fucker."

The redhead glanced our way and smiled.

"Like I said, I have a friend—"

"About time." I raised my chin in greeting.

"She's actually my partner's daughter."

Skintight Jimi Hendrix tee, camouflage shorts that left little to the imagination, and army boots.

"She has a problem."

I could definitely see myself standing at attention in front of her. "Is it that you're her friend?"

"It's…well, it's in your line of work."

"Did I mention I'm on vacation?"

"I'm actually a little surprised you haven't spotted her yet."

That jerked me out of my lecherous thoughts. "Her?"

Please be the redhead.

Please be the redhead.

Please be the redhead.

"Everyone else in the bar has." He pointed to the area behind me.

I glanced over my shoulder, spotted a blonde sitting in the corner booth, then turned toward her slowly, my jaw going slack as recognition sent a shockwave rocketing through my body. "That's her," I said, disbelief softening my voice. "That's the undermedicated gas pump lady."

I turned back to see Jason wearing that same shit-eating grin. "Yeah, I thought you might have been talking about her."

"You knew I was talking about your partner's daughter?"

"Not at first," he said, offended.

"Wait, you have a partner?"

"The blond hair and black Chevy single cab clued me in."

"When did you get a partner?"

"She's been through a lot."

I gave up trying to distract him and decided to take a more proactive approach. "Does she always come unhinged that easily?"

He stared at me to make sure he had my attention, then said again, "She's been through a lot."

Fucking hell. I turned back to her. She sat in a corner booth bathed in sunlight, head down, nose buried in a book, impervious to the hustle and bustle around her. Men cast interested glances her way while their dates glared.

Betty set a cup of hot tea on her table, a tell-tale string and tag hanging over the side of the thick mug. She followed it with what looked like a pastry, as though the woman were sitting in a coffee shop and not a rowdy, testosterone-filled bar.

But it didn't take long for me to glimpse a flaw in the picturesque scene or notice her shaking hands. Her chewed nails. She set the book down and picked up the tea, and I thought for a moment she might drop the mug.

"What's going on?" I asked, hating myself for it. I was the last person on Earth who could help someone. Most of my attempts at heroism failed. Miserably. This would be no different. "And what does my particular set of skills," I continued, managing to keep a straight face, "have to do with it?"

"If I were saying this to anyone else…" Jason began but paused, so I turned back to him. He tapped an irregular rhythm on the table—his nervous tic—before trying again. "She's being haunted."

I narrowed my eyes.

"Has been since she was a kid."

"Are you punking me right now? Because I swear to God—"

He held up a hand to stop me. "I know how it sounds. But you, of all people, should understand."

"I of all people?" I resisted the urge to grind my teeth to dust.

"Come on, man." He collapsed against the back of his chair. "You know about this shit. You can see things others can't."

I released a long breath and stated a simple fact. "She's not being haunted."

"I didn't think so at first either."

"She's not being haunted," I reiterated.

"I've seen the evidence. There's no other way to explain it."

"She's not being haunted," I said yet again, dropping my voice to a dangerous level.

"Why?" he shouted, alarming everyone around us.

Betty looked over in concern.

He shook his head at her, but he also caught the blonde's attention. She looked up from her book, a delicate line forming between her brows as she tried to figure out what was going on.

I turned my back to her and ducked my head, hoping to avoid her wrath. She was like a demon in sheep's clothing. I scowled at Jason.

"Why?" Jason asked, softer this time.

"It doesn't work like that."

"What do you mean?"

I rubbed my eyes with one hand—it had been a long two days—and refocused on him, wrangling my patience and putting it to good use. It wasn't Jason's fault that he didn't understand my fucked-up world. Few of the populace did. "I'm not saying people can't be haunted. Departed are pretty much everywhere, and poltergeists are straight-up assholes, but the departed don't generally fuck with the living. Most of them couldn't even if they wanted to." I didn't mention the fact that poltergeists pretty much lived—metaphorically—to fuck with the living. Mostly, because the odds of her having an actual poltergeist were astronomical. When he frowned, trying to process my meaning, I explained further. "Whatever is going on with her, it's most likely not supernatural."

After all, I'd seen her temper. She'd proven her stability issues to me only an hour earlier. Not that one thing couldn't lead to another or vice versa. Could her genuinely being haunted lead to other problems? A decline in physical and mental well-being? Of course. It just wasn't likely. Most often, the person was delusional to begin with.

It was nothing to be ashamed of. I knew more about mental disorders than most. I also knew more about the paranormal underworld than most, hence my plan to run for the border.

"I saw a video," Jason said as if that cleared everything right up.

"Because those can't be manipulated."

"Dude." He scrubbed his face and growled in frustration. "Why would she even do that?"

"You forget, I've seen her Jekyll and Hyde routine."

"Yes, but why?" he pleaded. "What would she have to gain? She lost her shit when she found out I'd seen the video."

I nodded. "That, I can believe."

He jolted forward, hope alight in his eyes. "You believe me about the ghost?"

"No, I've seen her lose her shit. I believe that part."

He collapsed again. It was like watching a soap opera. "She doesn't want anyone to know, so why create a video proving she has a ghost? Or a poltergeist. Or whatever you call it."

"Fine," I said, giving an inch. "Let's say a departed has attached itself to her. Or to something she has. What am I supposed to do about it?"

"You're asking me?" He paused to gape at me before adding, "You're the one who deals with this shit on a daily basis."

"Not daily," I said, pouting a bit.

He deadpanned me, his disbelief shining through in brilliant Technicolor.

"It's more like every other day."

He continued to stare until I caved.

"Okay, it's daily, but it's not all bad. It's just so…daily."

"All I'm saying is that she's had it rough. She's been terrorized by this thing since she was a kid. And she's dealt with it on her own." He tossed a glance her way, and I saw sympathy shimmering behind the mask of coolness he wore twenty-four-seven. "Her parents didn't believe her either."

I raised the cage around my heart. Reinforced it with barbed wire and steel. This was not my problem. "And she told you all of this?"

"No." He shook his head, his mouth thinning into a grim line. "She won't talk about it. Not even with the countless therapists and counselors her parents forced her to see for years. Her father told me. He's at his wit's end."

"So, he magically believes her now?"

"He does. Her mother did, too, before she died last year. Halle is all Donald has left."

"Donald?"

"Nordstrom. My business partner and the money behind all of this." He spread his arms, indicating the popular bar and grill.

I leaned closer and said softly, "It still doesn't mean she's being haunted by anything other than her own mind."

"I know," he said, conceding the point. "Just talk to her, okay? Read her aura—"

"Her what?"

"—and decide for yourself."

I pinched the bridge of my nose. If she weren't being ghosted—literally—then she was one hundred percent certifiable, and there was little I could do about either. Just because I could see the departed now didn't mean I had the skills to deal with them. They were more stubborn than the living. The fact that they were still on this plane when they should've crossed was proof of that. And they rarely left, even when I asked nicely.

"Time is running out," he added.

"What do you mean?"

He lowered his voice, his brows drawn into a severe line. "She tried to kill herself a couple of years ago."

I stared at him, the image of that ethereal creature trying to end her life throwing a left hook at my heart. Throwing and *landing* with his next words.

"And her father is convinced she's about to go for round two."

Chapter Two

And the award for
Chump of the Year goes to…
—T-shirt

Don't do it.

Jason's words hit like a forty-five-caliber round to my chest. Emotion seared across my skin and burned the backs of my eyes. A bit dramatic, maybe, but holy shit. Not only had I been duped, tricked into coming to Idaho—a fact that stunned me more than I cared to admit—but I'd also been lured into an impossible situation.

Don't do it.

Part of me wanted to rip my best friend's head off. He had no right to lay this on me. But I quickly made a mental U-turn. Out of every man in the bar—short, tall, beefy, small—Jason Vigil was the only one who could very likely take me in a bare-knuckle brawl. We'd both been boxers in high school, trading off championships like a baseball fan trades cards. We'd graduated to mixed martial arts soon after. Even then, I'd hated fighting Jason. We were too close, brothers, and I'd always wondered if he pulled his punches.

I didn't want to find out. Not now. And I didn't want to discover which of us had weathered our respective years best. If things didn't go as planned, I would be humiliated for the second time that day, and my self-esteem could only take so many hits.

Not to mention the fact that I couldn't throw a punch anymore to save my life. I couldn't fight if I wanted to. I was absolutely useless.

Don't do it.

Despite my best efforts, my gaze flitted to the girl. Her haunted expression didn't sway me. Didn't even nudge the needle. I didn't care if she'd been terrorized for years. That she looked as thin and frail as a paper doll. That she'd tried to take her life. I was done. Done with ghosts. Done with hellhounds. Done with demons—especially demons. Fuckers. None of it mattered. None of it was my problem. Not anymore. Even when she looked up from her book, her gaze meeting mine, and I found myself treading frantically just to keep my head above the murky depths I found there. I didn't budge.

Don't do it.

"You seem upset."

I turned back to Jason and quickly reassessed my chances of getting in a kidney punch before he took me to the mat. If I was certain I could take the shot, which I wasn't, I may have tried. "You think?"

The muscles in Jason's jaw tightened, and he leaned forward onto his elbows. "I'm sorry."

"About which part? The luring me here under false pretenses bit, or the fact that you're ruining my vacation?"

"Neither." He pointed over my shoulder. "I think she recognized you."

I whirled around.

She was headed our way, carrying the mug and her book.

"That's my cue." Jason flew out of his chair and booked it to the kitchen. Cowardly bastard.

The seat he'd vacated didn't stay empty for long. Before I could get up and run myself—I said he was a cowardly bastard, not that I wasn't—she sank into Jason's chair, folding her long legs as gracefully as a fawn settling onto a forest floor.

"It's you," she said, clearly just as surprised to see me as I was to see her. She put the mug and book on the table, apparently planning to stay a while.

Why did she seem so fragile now, when I would've sworn she was seconds away from chopping me to pieces with a battle axe an hour ago? Why were her features so much more delicate? Her eyes so much more expressive? And blue. The smooth, cobalt blue of a ceramic bowl. Had they been this blue before? Or did they change with her moods?

Either way, her father was right. She would choose a period over a pause, though not for a few months. Only this time, she would succeed. I saw her last moment—chewed nails, limp hands, wrists open—in a bathtub soaked with blood, her bent knees protruding out of the water. November 12th. 8:28 p.m.

For the love of God, Eric, don't fucking do it. If you fail, and you will *fail…*

No. Just no. There was nothing I could do. I could not take this on. I *would* not take this on. I'd text Jason the details of her death so her father could stop it and be on my merry way before anyone—namely, my friend—even knew I'd left.

I shook out of my thoughts, nodded a greeting that served as both hello and goodbye, and started to rise. But before I could take my leave, the tinny voice of an elderly woman drifted toward me—one who'd died in her sixties sometime *in* the sixties.

"I like her," she said, beaming at the oblivious blonde.

With a heavy sigh, I sank back into the seat and cast a sideways glance at my boss's aunt, always impressed with how much her blue hair glowed, even in the afterlife. At some point before her death, Aunt Lillian—as she'd insisted I call her—had been swallowed whole by one of those floral tents. She wore an impressive array of love beads and had a brown leather strap tied around her wrist.

I'd asked her once how she died. She'd mentioned a hippie commune, a love affair with a bona fide shaman, and a bad batch of LSD. My only disappointment when I first met her was that she didn't have a peace sign painted on her cheek.

"She seems sad, though," Aunt Lil continued.

"How did you recognize me?" I asked Halle, ignoring the woman who'd followed me all the way from Santa Fe. "I was wearing a helmet."

Halle pointed. "The New Mexico shirt with the *Breaking Bad* RV is hard to forget."

"Right."

She dropped her gaze, denying me the pleasure of looking into her blue irises for a few painful seconds. "I'm sorry. About the convenience store. I thought my houseboat was on fire and didn't have enough gas to make it to the marina."

"Why?"

She looked up, and the air fled from my lungs. "Because my truck was on empty."

"What? No. I meant why did you think your houseboat was on fire?"

"Oh, I got an alert on my phone. I panicked and took it out on you. I just want you to know I've never done anything like that before. Not ever," she added when I eyed her doubtfully. "I swear."

I studied the dark circles under her eyes, her chapped lips, her nails that had been chewed raw, and fought the concern inching up my chest.

"Not once." She pulled her lower lip between her teeth and reopened a small cut that had been healing before adding, "In my life."

"I know what never means," I said, pretending to be unmoved and wondering if I should apologize for revving my engine every time she tried to talk.

"I believe her," Aunt Lil said. She nudged me. Or she would have if she weren't incorporeal. Instead, her elbow slid across my arm like a shadow. "I think we should take her case, Constantine."

I closed my eyes and prayed for patience.

"I'm sorry to have bothered you." Halle grabbed her book and mug and started to leave.

"What kind of security system alerts you that your house is on fire?" I asked, interrupting her departure.

"Excuse me?"

"I've never heard of a home security app doing that."

She sat down again. "Oh, yeah." She pulled her phone out of a small bag slung over one shoulder and started to show me but then seemed to change her mind. "Well, it's supposed to. But mine… Security systems don't like me in general, but this was a first. I've never gotten a fire alert."

"Then your houseboat wasn't on fire?"

"No. And let me tell you, the firefighters who showed up were not happy."

"Firemen!" Aunt Lillian said, perking up. "I wonder if they were hot."

I laughed softly for Halle's benefit, not Aunt Lillian's. I didn't dare encourage the woman. "You would think they'd be happy—"

"Ask her if they were hot."

"—not having to fight a fire and all."

"You'd think," Halle said. "You're Jason's friend?"

"The one and only," I said, offering her a grin.

She smiled, just barely, and the Earth stopped spinning on its axis for several precious seconds. A thousand years from now, all the clocks would be wrong, thanks to that hiccup. This would throw everything off.

"My dad told me about you. Jason has him convinced you're the real deal."

"The real deal?"

"That you can see into the supernatural world."

"Oh!" Aunt Lil said, squirming in a chair that just happened to be pulled out enough for her to pretend to squeeze into it. "Tell her about me!"

"Jason's a pathological liar."

A dimple appeared at one corner of her mouth. Amazing how something so small could shake me so hard. "I've heard that about him."

She wrapped both hands around the mug and took a sip of tea as though bracing herself for her next words. "You helped me," she said after swallowing hard. "At the gas station, you helped me get that pump, even after I treated you so horrendously. Why?"

"I'm a member of the Knights in Shining Armor Club. It's mandatory that we help one maiden in distress a day or we lose our parking privileges."

She pursed her lips, trying to keep a wayward grin at bay. "You don't say."

"We also get a ten-percent discount at Cracker Barrel."

This time, she laughed—a beautiful, lyrical sound that…

Holy fuck, I had to stop. This was getting ridiculous. I needed to get out of here before I dropped to one knee and proposed. I scanned the bar. Wasn't there a redhead around here somewhere? Someone, anyone to take my mind off Halle Nordstrom.

"Do you really have experience with all that stuff?"

I refocused on her and absently lifted a shoulder. "There are few people on the planet with more." Besides some of my closest friends, but that was a story for another day.

The heat from Aunt Lil's glare almost seared the flesh off my face. "You're not going to tell her about me, are you?"

"Jason says you can even see when people are going to die."

I rolled my eyes. Did that asshole spill all my secrets?

"You're ashamed of me, aren't you?" Aunt Lil pouted, crossing her arms over her muumuu-clad chest.

"So, what?" Halle asked with a soft laugh to lighten her next question. "You're like…the grim reaper?"

"No, but she's a good friend of mine."

Her mouth formed a hesitant grin. "You say the funniest things."

"Well, I'm also a member of the National Association for the Fair and Ethical Treatment of Stand-up Comedians, so…"

I saw she wanted to laugh but couldn't quite manage it. Her next question seemed to weigh too heavily on her mind. She stuck a chewed fingernail between her teeth and asked softly, "Can you see when I'm going to die?"

I shook my head. "Sorry."

"And now you're lying to her." Aunt Lil tsked at me.

"It comes and goes," I added, lying my ass off.

"Ah." Relief softened the convex curve of Halle's shoulders, a reaction I didn't expect. But, of course, she would be relieved. She didn't want me to throw a wrench into her final plans.

But again, none of this was my problem. I only helped those in immediate danger, and even then, it had to be a life-or-death situation. Something I couldn't fuck up too badly. Halle may very well be haunted, though I still had my doubts, but I could hardly do anything about it either way. Her impending doom could be thwarted with good timing and a little luck, so my job here was done. Now, to leave. Get up and say my goodbyes. How hard could it be?

"Are you really going to ignore me all night, Constantine?"

Why did Aunt Lil love my middle name so much? I started to cast her a quick scowl to shush her—not that my threats ever worked—but changed my mind. Maybe she was my ticket out of this situation. My escape. Perhaps I didn't have to leave after all and look like an asshole—not that I wasn't. I just needed to scare Halle off so she did the leaving.

I pulled my mouth into a calculated smile, turned, and looked straight at Aunt Lil. "Did your niece send you to watch over me?"

Aunt Lil stared at me, her lids fluttering in confusion. "My niece?"

"You remember her. Charley Davidson? The saucy one with brown hair and a killer dropkick?"

She came to her senses and crossed her arms over her love beads. "So, we're on speaking terms again?"

"What are you doing?" Halle asked, her expression wary.

"Oh." I bounced back to her. "Sorry. Remember that supernatural realm I can see into? Well, my boss's aunt, who died in the sixties from a hit of acid—"

"That was such a bad trip."

"—was apparently sent to spy on me." I turned my best accusing glare on her. "Isn't that right, Aunt Lillian?"

The woman turned and raised a hand to summon a server, forgetting she couldn't.

I leaned closer. "Good luck with that."

"Are you making fun of me?" Halle asked.

"What? Not at all. My boss's aunt is sitting right here."

Halle raised her chin and curled her fingers around her book, readying to leave.

This had worked so much better than I'd thought it would. "So, you're being haunted but don't believe in ghosts?"

"You're intimidating her, Constantine," Aunt Lil chided.

"No, I do," Halle said. "I also know when I've become the butt of a joke." The pain that flickered across her face was almost my undoing.

"Whatever my father is paying you—"

"That's not what this is..." Her words sank in, and I glanced up in surprise. "He's paying me?"

She smiled and said softly, "Not anymore."

Jason didn't mention anything about money. He probably planned to keep it for himself. The bastard.

"Besides," Halle continued, her tone resigned, "some people deserve to be haunted."

What did that mean? "What does that mean?" I asked her shapely backside as she strutted away, her powder blue sundress flowing like water down the backs of her legs.

Aunt Lil tsked me again, her disappointment evident in her glower. "That could've gone better."

"Actually, it went exactly as planned." But why did I feel like such a jerk? "Wait, did Charley really send you?"

She winced and looked around. "Where's a barmaid when you need one?"

A barmaid. I scoffed until the word *bar* reminded me. I jumped to my feet and scanned the area. "Fuck. Where'd the kid go?"

"What kid?" Aunt Lil asked.

I spotted Jason and rushed over to him, almost taking out two of his customers in the process.

"How'd it go?" he asked, that shit-eating grin right where I'd left it.

"Where's the kid?"

He was filling a beer glass from the tap. "What kid?"

"The one with the denim jacket." I gestured toward the empty barstool then scanned the area again.

"Oh, he ordered a ride." He set the glass in front of a scruffy biker wearing a pink bandana, shoved a hand into his pocket, and pulled out a set of keys, dangling them in front of me like a kid playing keep-away. "He won't be driving anywhere today."

I spun back to the table. The clean table that a group of college kids had already taken. The redhead was walking away with a tray full of napkins, empty bottles, and a coffee mug.

"Wait!" I hurried over to her, searched the tray for my napkin, and bolted back to Jason, cringing about the fact that I had to ignore the blinding smile the redhead flashed me.

Another time. Definitely another time.

I showed the napkin to Jason. "Where is this?"

He tilted his head and frowned. "I think the question you need to ask is *what* is this?"

I turned the napkin this way and that, trying to make out the drawing myself. "Damn it. I don't know. I think it's a bridge, maybe?"

He stepped closer. "How is that a bridge?"

"It looks like it could be one. See these pillar things?"

"Pillar things?" he asked, unimpressed.

Betty peeked around Jason's shoulder. "That's the Arkwright Building in Spokane."

We turned to her in unison.

"Are you sure?" I asked, checking my watch. Forty-three minutes. How far was Spokane from here?

"Yeah, it's gorgeous. Very historic. Those are the columns out front," she said, pointing to the pillar things. "And this part here? That's the balcony on the second floor above the entrance if you're looking up. But I don't think it's a real balcony," she said to Jason then gazed at me in admiration. "The perspective is spot on, though. Good job."

If she only knew. Then again, with Jason spilling all my secrets to anyone within shouting distance, maybe she did know. "Thanks." I took out my phone and entered the Arkwright Building into my maps app.

"What's going on?" Jason asked.

"Remember how I told you I can tell the exact moment someone is going to die?"

Three people close by swiveled their heads to gawk at me. It happened.

"Zachary?" Jason asked, knowing the answer. The blood drained from his face.

Betty looked concerned, too. "It makes sense. His dad works maintenance there."

I raked a hand through my hair. "So, he would have access to the roof."

"Absolutely."

I glanced at my watch again.

"How much time do we have?" Jason asked.

"We?"

He nodded and dug into his pocket for another set of keys. "I'll drive."

"You've been drinking," Betty said, her expression soft but as hard as marble. There would be no arguments brooked on her watch.

"I can drive you."

We all turned to see Halle standing there. She held up a twenty. "I forgot to pay so I came back." Her gaze flitted to me then darted away just as quickly. "I haven't had anything to drink. We can take my truck."

It looked like I had little choice. "Will it get me there in forty-two minutes?"

The smug countenance that spread across her face almost doubled me over. She stole a line from one of my favorite movies and said, "Which floor?"

Chapter Three

It's never as funny to the police as it is to us.
—Meme

Dominic Toretto had nothing on Halle Nordstrom. She weaved in and out of traffic like a street racer on speed. Unfortunately, we'd hit rush hour, so there was a lot of weaving.

The first few minutes of the drive were utterly silent. I didn't want to distract her, which was a great excuse to keep my mouth shut. I had no idea what to say anyway. But once she made it to the main highway, she relaxed and instigated the conversation herself.

"So, this kid. He's going to die soon?"

I checked my watch yet again and tried to keep my adrenaline from spiraling out of control. "Yes. Very."

She nodded in thought, then asked, "Do you know how?"

"Yes, and no. I don't know if he's going to jump or fall. It could be an accident. He had a lot to drink."

The quick look she cast my way was full of fear. "Should we call the cops?"

I winced. The police and I didn't always see eye to eye. They tended to complicate things. Asked questions like, "Where did you get this information?" and "How did you know she was going to be murdered with a hacksaw before it happened?" I learned early on not to rely on them.

"They could beat us there," she argued. "They could stop him if we don't make it."

She was right, of course. I nodded. "We should try to get ahold of his dad, too." I took out my phone to text Jason for the contact info while Halle talked to the cops.

"I don't know," she said to dispatch, feigning hysterics. At least, I *hoped* she was feigning. "I just saw a kid on the roof like he was going to jump! Please hurry!" She hung up before they could ask her anything else.

"You've had acting experience?"

She smirked. "Haven't we all?"

Right again. "Think they'll send someone?"

"I hope so."

I studied her profile for a minute, like the alabaster statue of a wood sprite. My phone dinged, and I tore my gaze off her. "Jason's been trying to get ahold of the dad. He's not picking up." I checked my watch. "How much longer?"

"Ten minutes," she said, swerving onto the shoulder to maneuver around a truck.

My stomach clenched tighter with every second that passed.

Once we were back on the actual highway, she tossed me an apologetic grin. "Make that nine."

"And you were a stunt driver in a past life?"

"Sorry. I won't do that unless I absolutely have to. It's too risky. If we get pulled over now… Let me know if you see a cop."

"Will do," I said, my voice suddenly hoarse. "I thought you didn't believe me."

"I don't, but I also don't want to be responsible for someone's death if I could've done something about it and didn't."

"Welcome to my world," I said with a breathy scoff. I'd never asked for any of this shit. Fucking demon.

We exited the freeway and hit downtown Spokane at the height of rush hour. Bumper-to-bumper traffic brought us to a standstill, and my lungs fought for air.

"I forgot about the hour." She glanced around, looking for a quicker route before pulling half onto a sidewalk, throwing her truck into park, and pointing out the windshield. "That's the building. It's only a couple more blocks." She turned the full force of an imploring gaze on me. "We have to run for it."

The fact that she wore a sundress and sandals did not escape me.

Apparently, it didn't escape her either. She opened her truck door, then looked back. "Don't wait for me."

"You sure?" I asked over the hood once I got out.

She nodded and gathered the folds of her skirt. "Go."

I took off and didn't look back, wending through pedestrians and vehicles alike until I came to the exact spot I'd seen in Zachary's last moment. I peered up. Seven stories never looked so high.

"Here!" Halle said, rushing past me and into the building as the first drops of rain began to fall.

"How the hell—?"

"There's an elevator!" She pointed and ran toward it.

As though a gift from the gods, the doors were already open. We tumbled inside, both of us struggling to fill our lungs, and then I remembered. "That's right. It was raining in his final moment."

She cast me a startled expression and pushed the button for the top floor. Our breaths synced, creating a rhythm in the quiet elevator.

"You're fast," I said between gasps.

She put a hand to her racing heart. "You're faster. I could hardly keep up."

"But you did. I'm impressed."

"Those four years of track must've paid off."

Apparently.

We bolted out of the elevator the second the doors opened and rushed up a set of stairs to the roof access. The steel door wasn't locked, and I thanked the powers that be for small favors. When we burst through the door with guns blazing—metaphorically—we almost took out a uniformed cop.

"Officer," Halle said, stopping short in surprise.

I checked my watch and ran past him. Three minutes.

"Did you make the call?" he asked Halle.

I didn't hear her reply. I sprinted to the middle of the rooftop and did a three-sixty, but the only other person on the roof was a burly maintenance man, his gray shirt spotted with fresh raindrops.

"Are you Eric?" he asked as he walked toward me. Clearly, Jason had gotten ahold of Zachary's dad.

"I am."

"I'm Bobby." He took my hand. "I don't know what's going on, but Zachary isn't here."

Fuck. Did he jump already? No way. He couldn't have. The time thing was never wrong unless… Unless he jumped but didn't die when he landed. If it took him a few minutes to pass, for his heart to stop beating, I wouldn't see the actual jump. I would only see when his soul left his body.

I turned back to Bobby. "Which side is the front of the building?"

He pointed to my right. I rushed to the edge and looked over. A ledge capped the sixth level of the historic brick building with just enough depth for a person to walk on. No Zachary. And no body on the ground. I spun around, confused, then looked at my watch. Two minutes. What the hell?

The cop's voice broke through my panicked thoughts. "I don't know what you saw, ma'am, but I have another call. Someone parked a pickup on the sidewalk a couple of blocks away, and apparently, the world's gonna end."

Halle's eyes rounded. She brushed a lock of damp blond hair off her face and stuck a chewed fingernail between her teeth again. "That's so weird. Why would someone do that?"

The cop handed her his card with a tip of his hat and a friendly smile. "If you need anything else, ma'am." Too friendly.

Was he flirting? At a time like this?

Bobby looked over the edge, too, trying to figure out what was going on. "Did Zach say something to you? Jason didn't really tell me much."

"Did you find him?" Halle asked. The cop left, and she walked over to us.

I shook my head.

She frowned and glanced around. "You saw him jump from here?"

"Jump?" Bobby asked.

"No." I ground my teeth and did another three-sixty. "I see the last moment from the person's perspective. It's about a three-second window before and after the soul leaves the body. He was definitely falling. I saw windows above him, and the balcony and pillars right before everything went black."

Halle nodded. "Then that's the only explanation, right?"

"It has to be." We sprinted to the other side, frantically searching for the kid.

"I want to know what's going on," Bobby said, fear giving his baritone voice an unnatural quaver. "Who's jumping?"

"Bobby, does Zach ever come up here? You know, just to chill?"

The man was out of breath and went into a slight state of shock when our words started to sink in. "He…he does, but he likes to climb over the ladder and sit on the ledge."

Halle looked at him in horror. "Who does that?"

"He loves heights," Bobby said as though that explained everything.

One minute.

The skies opened up, and raindrops began falling freely, the rooftop suddenly slick as I hurried to the other side and looked over. When I still didn't see him, I closed my eyes and fought to remember Zach's last moment once more. What was I missing?

The windows.

The balcony.

The columns.

And I got the feeling of movement like he was falling, but backward. For him to be able to see what he saw, he would've fallen backward. Who jumped off a roof backward?

I felt a hand on my arm and lifted my lids to see Halle beside me, her face full of hope. "You can do this," she said, and I realized she was shivering, her lips turning blue in the rain. She squinted against the icy drops as they pelted her face.

The rain. The limited vision. I looked over the edge once more. The rush-hour traffic.

The truth hit me like a midsection punch from Iron Mike. I was in the wrong place. I lifted my wrist and wiped rain off my watch. And I was out of time.

Without another thought, I ran to the access door. I heard Halle behind me. I yelled, "Take the elevator!" as I bounded down the stairs in a single leap. Then I did the same to both sets of stairs per level until I hit the bottom floor.

Praying no one was on the other side, I burst through the door, splintering the wood and breaking the handle. It slammed against the wall so hard the building vibrated as I ran through the business space on the bottom floor and shoved my way through glass doors onto the street.

Knowing which direction Zachary would be coming from—the only direction he could, considering his last moment—I spotted him crossing the street instantly. I also saw the delivery truck, seconds away from running him down.

I reacted without thinking. Later, I would come to regret that, but for now, my legs carried me with only one thought in mind: *Get that kid out of harm's way*. I tackled him and turned just as the truck slammed into us. Me. While I'd pushed Zachary out of the truck's path, I'd put myself in it, but I was apparently prepared for just such a scenario. I raised a hand and shoved off the fender, managing to avoid a head-on and getting a gentle, bone-rattling sideswipe instead.

I didn't feel a thing as the truck tossed me like a ragdoll in the opposite direction Zachary would have flown. Unfortunately, that was straight into more traffic. I barely registered screeching tires, horns, and a scream before the world went black.

Half an hour later, I sat in the back of an ambulance, trying to convince the first responder I was okay.

She was cute. And she really wanted my pants off.

"They're half-ripped off anyway," she said, defending her position.

They weren't just half off. They were shredded, my *Breaking Bad* tee a sad homage to Walter's last days, but my injuries weren't that bad. Scrapes and bruises and possibly a mild concussion. Either that or Halle was really gazing at me with doe-like eyes full of both concern and gratitude. She sat beside the EMT, wringing her hands. And still shivering.

"I really think you should go to the hospital," the med-tech said.

"Can I get a blanket?" I asked her.

"Of course." She rose to her feet and brought down a blue blanket wrapped in plastic. She unwrapped it and started to lay it over me, but I sat up, took it from her, and draped it over Halle's shoulders.

Halle fought me. Naturally. "I'm fine. You need this more than I do."

I tugged it tightly around her and held the ends in a clenched fist, daring her to get it off. She was soaked to the bone and had just saved a life. I wouldn't have made it in time without her help. And her erratic driving. She deserved a warm blanket.

"Is he okay?" the truck driver asked for the fiftieth time. "My damn defroster doesn't work. I've told my company a dozen times." He scraped a hand down his face and walked off when he got a call.

"How did you get down there so fast?" Bobby asked. He was standing in the rain, holding onto his son with an arm over his shoulders. "I've never seen anything like it."

"Adrenaline?" I guessed. Though the long legs didn't hurt.

"You saved my life," Zachary said, and I couldn't be certain he wasn't still drunk. His words were slightly slurred, either from the alcohol earlier or the cold. As warm as the day had been, the rain felt like an ice storm in January.

I grinned at him. "Can I ask you something, kid?"

He winced at my use of the word *kid*, but I had a decade on him, and I was going to use it.

"Why were you drinking so much?"

His eyes widened, and he cast a sideways glance at his dad before asking, "You mean at the bar?"

I nodded as the EMT irrigated one of my deeper scrapes before placing a piece of gauze on top and wrapping it.

"What are you talking about?" Bobby asked him. "How much did you drink?"

Zachary cleared his throat. "A lot. I had something to tell you, and I didn't know how."

Bobby eased his hold to face him. "What's going on?"

"First," Zachary said, taking a cautionary step backward. This would be good. "Just know I'm going to finish college, okay? If it's the last thing I do, I'll get my degree."

"Okay," his dad said, his voice and expression wary. "And second?"

Zachary kicked a rock. "Second, Teresa's pregnant."

Bobby's jaw fell open as Zachary kicked another pebble and looked away. After taking a moment to absorb that bombshell, Bobby pressed his lips together and patted his son's shoulder. "It's okay."

"No, it's not. Mom is gonna freak."

"True, but we'll talk to her together."

Seeing their close bond warmed my heart. Not like…a lot, though. Maybe a twelfth of a degree.

"Wait," Bobby said, scratching his neck in thought. "I thought your girlfriend's name was Lauren."

Zachary stuffed his hands into his pockets and said, "It is."

"Then who's Teresa?"

Zachary cleared his throat, then said softly, "Lauren's sister."

Halle gasped then turned to me and patted my arm, pretending not to hear. "Maybe we should head back now."

"I think that's a good idea." I hustled off the gurney despite the EMT's protests.

"I don't know how to thank you," Zachary said.

Finishing college would not be the last thing he did. I saw his new-and-improved last moment, and it would not happen for a very long time—though still too young in my book.

"You could lay off the carbs," I suggested.

I waited a few seconds then looked again. Damn it. No one ever took dieting advice to heart. He would die in his late sixties of cardiac arrest. In his defense, most of the last moments I saw were practically cemented in stone, which was why I rarely tried to change history. Today's outcome was unusual.

"I still think you should go to the hospital," the EMT said, adopting a childlike posture complete with crossed arms and a protruding lower lip.

"It's okay. I think we have a pickup to get out of impound." I eased out of the ambulance and turned to help Halle down.

"Oh, your blanket," she said to the EMT, handing it back to her. "Thank you."

The woman accepted it with a deeper pout.

Fortunately, we found Halle's pickup before the tow truck arrived. While she distracted the cop, I hopped into the cab and took off. The officer gave a half-hearted pursuit before giving up and going back for more one-on-one time with Halle. Sadly, in a stranger-than-fiction turn of events, she vanished when he got a call over his radio, never to be seen or heard from again. At least by the cop. He could run her tags and make the connection, but she hadn't really broken any laws. She was simply reclaiming the pickup she'd parked badly. And she hadn't actually done the take back. It had been practically stolen out from under her by a maniac in a shredded shirt and ripped jeans.

After years of practice, I could run defensive scenarios all day.

I tightened my grip on the steering wheel and looked over at Halle. She was still shivering, and I didn't know if it was due to her dress and hair still being damp or the accident she'd witnessed. The Arkwright Building must have the fastest elevator in all of Washington. She and Bobby had made it down just in time to watch me play tag with a delivery truck.

I blasted the heater as we drove, the setting sun creating bright splashes of pink and orange in the rearview. "Can I ask you a question?"

She was chewing on her lower lip as she stared at my leg. Or, more precisely, the super cool wound there.

I slid a hand over it, suddenly self-conscious.

She snapped to attention with my question. "Sure."

"What did you mean, some people deserve to be haunted?"

"Oh," she said, surprised. She hugged herself and looked out the window. "Nothing. You may not believe this, but I haven't always been a good person."

"You're right. I don't believe it."

She turned to me suddenly, huffing out an exasperated puff of air. "Can we just address the elephant in the room?"

"I didn't realize there was one."

She shifted in her seat to face me head-on. "How?"

"Well, first, we aren't even in a room, so I don't think my not noticing the elephant in it is the most pertinent element of this conversation."

"No, I mean…you really knew."

Ah. That.

"You knew the exact date, time, and place Zachary was going to die."

I held up a finger to put her on pause. "Not the place, just the date and time."

"But you saw it. You were able to figure out where he was from what you saw. How?" She dropped her gaze, racking her brain. "How is that even possible?"

"Well, I could tell you, but then I'd have to kill you, dismember your lifeless body, and bury you in Jason's backyard."

"Can you…can you really talk to dead people?"

"Tell her!" Aunt Lil said. She was sitting between us in the cramped cab, making the situation fairly awkward as I tried to look at Halle from around her blue hair. "We need to help her. If she's being terrorized, we're all she's got, Constantine."

"Yes, I can. Aunt Lil is here now."

Halle reared back, though just barely before catching herself. She squinted and looked around, trying to peer into the veil as I fought a grin. "Can she hear me?"

"Yes."

"Tell her she has a lovely voice."

I gave up and let the grin get a solid foothold. "Aunt Lil likes your voice," I relayed.

"Oh." Halle sat up straighter. "Thank you."

"Okay," Aunt Lil said, clapping soundlessly, "my job here is done. I'm going to go check out that hottie at the bar some more. He may like Betty, but she ain't got a ring on her finger yet. Am I right?"

She disappeared before I could answer.

Halle folded her hands in her lap. "It's very nice to meet you, Lillian."

Should I tell her?

"I hope we can become friends."

This was getting awkward. "She's gone."

"Really?" Her shoulders dropped. "I had so many questions."

"She does that. Pops in and out like a loose lightbulb. It's okay until she decides to ride sidesaddle in my lap on the bike. I almost died making this trip. Twice."

She laughed softly, the sound like a summer breeze. "Where did she go?"

"To stalk Jason."

She laughed again. I was on a roll. "He probably deserves it."

"Agreed."

She smoothed the skirt of her dress and asked, "Have you always been able to do what you do? Like, since you were a kid?"

I thought for a moment before answering, wondering how much to tell her. They say honesty is the best policy, but I've found people don't really want to hear how bad they look in a swimsuit. "Since I was a kid? Yes, to a degree. But things became…amplified a handful of years ago."

"Amplified how?"

I took the exit that would lead us back to Cruisers and my bike. "Do you remember the weird outbreak that shut Albuquerque down about five years ago?"

She shot up again with the memory. "I do. That was bizarre. A virus caused people to go crazy and become violent overnight."

I clicked my tongue. "That's the one."

"They had to quarantine the whole city and then it just stopped."

"Thanks to a few of my closest friends."

"They stopped the virus?" she asked in awe.

"It was never a virus. It was supernatural in nature."

Her mouth rounded prettily. "I don't understand."

"Well, they kind of started it so it was pretty much up to them to stop it. The important thing is, they succeeded." When she simply watched me, waiting for more, I obliged. "These friends are supernatural entities themselves and kind of accidentally opened a hell dimension on Earth. The demons from that dimension possessed…certain people and turned them violent." She didn't need to know they only possessed people with mental illnesses. People like me. "I was one of them."

She sucked in a soft breath and then covered her mouth with both hands.

"One of my friends, one of the supernatural entities, was able to extricate the demon inside me, with the help of a departed Rottweiler named Artemis."

"Dogs can become ghosts, too?"

I laughed. She would focus on that part. "They can, though like humans, they usually cross."

She sank back in a stupor. "Dogs really do go to heaven?"

"I like to think there's a special one just for them."

"Why did it possess you? Was it a wrong-place-at-the-wrong-time kind of scenario?"

Back to the honesty thing. I'd come this far. May as well lay it all out on the table. I mustered all the courage my depleted stores had to offer and charged forward. "It took a while, but my friends figured out the demons from that particular dimension only possessed people… with a mental disorder." I circled an index finger around my ear to make light of that fact. "You know, the crazies."

I expected her complete and total withdrawal from the conversation. Instead, she tilted her head and studied me. "What kind of mental disorder?"

I checked the GPS. "Is it this turn or the next one?"

"Oh," she said as though suddenly realizing how close we were. She pointed. "This one."

With a nod of understanding, I turned left and then pulled into Cruisers about half a block later. I threw her truck into park and then turned to face her. "Thank you, Halle. Zachary wouldn't be alive right now if not for you."

"Yeah, well, you're the one who went head-to-head with a delivery truck."

She pressed her hands together in her lap as we sat, neither of us sure what to say. I was so bad with small talk. And since we were just sitting there with nothing to do, I took another look. Just a quick one. *Just* to make sure I didn't miss anything.

Since her impending death wasn't detrimentally close at hand, I had to actually concentrate to see her last moment. The closer the death was, the less I had to focus until it became overpowering. Like today with Zachary. The moment had shone brightly in my mind the second my gaze drifted anywhere near him. Times like those, I couldn't stop the visions if I wanted to, thus my obsession with the kid's inevitable demise.

But this time, I didn't stop the vision of Halle's last moment. Even though watching it was like a knife twisting painfully in my heart. I took my time and studied her surroundings. The red bathwater. The limp hands. The slit wrists. The image paralyzed my lungs, and I wanted to leave, but something from my first glimpse had been nagging me, niggling at the back of my mind. I needed to know what.

Then I saw it. A reflection in a mirror…

"Halle," I said, my voice barely more than a whisper. But before I could say anything else, a raucous cheer hit us, and patrons started streaming out of the bar, clapping, hooting, and hollering. They surrounded the truck and started banging on the hood in enthusiasm.

I rolled my eyes. I was going to kill him.

"Do you think they know?" Halle asked with a giggle.

I spotted Jason, his shit-eating grin full of pride. Did he tell the whole fucking town? "He is so dead."

Halle giggled again and got out of the truck as those around her offered to buy her a drink. An older gentleman pulled her into his arms and hugged her tightly. Had to be her father, Jason's partner.

Jason opened the driver's side door and hauled me out, but celebrating was about the last thing on my mind. All I could think about was Halle's last moment and the reflection in the mirror of a man's hand holding a straight razor.

Chapter Four

Don't judge.
I clean up real nice.
—T-shirt

I took small, leisurely sips of the beer I'd been given. The tenth one in two hours. I could only pass my glass to the person next to me so many times before someone noticed. The patrons were taking turns buying me drink after drink for saving Zachary's life.

According to Jason, I just happened to see Zachary crossing the busy intersection and noticed the truck bearing down on him. My lightning-quick reflexes took over, and I whisked him out of harm's way.

It was a complete coincidence we were in the same place at the same time, so Jason's ability to lie with a straight face saved him from the torment of my wrath yet again. Lucky bastard. So here I sat as person after person asked me to tell the story.

Halle was smart. She'd ducked out with her father ten minutes into the celebration when I went to change. She was probably on her houseboat right now, sleeping soundly. The mental image of her in a slinky nightgown, blond hair spilling over a pillow, long legs tangled in silk sheets, caused every blood cell in my body to rush to the more sensitive regions of my anatomy.

The redhead put yet another beer in front of me, her smile as sweet and inviting as a tangerine. Three hours ago, I would've jumped at the chance for some alone time with the stunner, but even then, it would have only been to get the blonde out of my head.

Jason came up behind me and slapped me on the back. Because I hadn't just been hit by a fucking truck. He laughed when I glared at him. "Looks like you robbed another grave today."

I took a pretend sip and questioned him. "What are you talking about?"

"You kept yet another body out of the ground. Your reputation remains intact, Grave Robber."

I tried not to roll my eyes. I failed. "That's a ridiculous nickname. And what does that have to do with anything?"

"Well, let's see." He looked up in thought. "You got the nickname when you punched an opponent in the solar plexus so hard he stopped breathing."

"I was there."

"And you fell to your knees, ripped off your gloves, and started doing CPR in the middle of the ring."

Too bad I hadn't thought to do that several years ago when I punched a man in a bar fight and knocked him unconscious. He later died. I had every intention of turning myself in, but the leader of the motorcycle club I belonged to, one of the best friends I've ever had, convinced me not to. Told me to lay low. As a result, a video of the incident showed up on our doorstep a few weeks later, and we were blackmailed into committing some pretty horrendous crimes. More importantly, I lost the ability to take a swing at anyone for any reason. I was supposedly destined through prophecy to fight in a war against Satan himself, but I could no longer fight. I was as useless as a knitted condom.

"I. Was. There," I reminded Jason. "And?"

"And today you robbed another grave."

"How do you figure that?" Thankfully, realization dawned before I looked like a complete idiot. "Oh, right. Zachary."

"See? Self-fulfilling prophecy."

"Let's not talk about prophecies."

"Whatev. When are you going to stop accepting beers you have no intention of drinking and get some rest?"

I shook my head. "Not just yet. I want Halle's address."

He scoffed. "Yeah, so does every other man in this bar."

I bit down and said under my breath, "She's in more trouble than you or I ever imagined."

He eased closer. "What do you mean?"

I moved even closer and said into his ear, "Unless I'm greatly mistaken—it happens—she's going to be murdered in about two months."

Jason stilled and studied me as though trying to figure out if I was kidding or not.

"I don't joke about death." When he continued to stare, I added, "I mean, I do, but I'm not joking about this. I would never."

"How?" he asked, his eyes glistening as emotion swelled inside him. As Halle's reality sank in. After a few seconds, anger took hold, and he asked from between clenched teeth, "Who?"

"I'll explain, but right now I need that address."

He nodded and said, "Give me a sec," before crossing the floor to his office.

I followed.

"Are you okay to drive your bike? I can get you a ride."

"I barely touched the beers they bought."

He passed me a piece of paper with Halle's address and a hand-drawn map of the slip she rented at the marina. "There's that, too, but you're pretty beat up. Your wounds looked serious."

"I've had worse. Trust me."

"I know. I was usually the one giving them to you, but this time is different."

"Not really. Being hit by you or a six-ton delivery truck feels startlingly similar."

"Vause," he said, not buying it.

"Vigil," I countered, relisting it and hoping he'd press the *buy it now* button.

"Fine," he said, caving. "Just be careful. And, please, get to the bottom of this before either of you gets killed."

I pointed a finger pistol at him and winked. "That's the plan, Stan."

"And don't call me Stan!" he shouted as I walked out.

Putting on my helmet proved far more painful than I ever imagined it would, and the real possibility of a subdural hematoma—I'd had several in my life—had me worried. Not, like, bad, but there was definitely a tinge of concern. Getting into my leather jacket was just as irksome. I would really feel that truck tomorrow.

As I drove down deserted streets and through shadowy trees to the marina, I thought of a hundred different scenarios that might explain the man in Halle's last moment. Could he be a departed? Yes. Since I could see the departed even in pictures and on film, he very well could be.

They were as plain to me as anything else in the shot, though their coloring was a little off and their images a little blurry. But the departed handling objects in the physical world was another story. Few could perform such tricks, and when they did, they usually couldn't do it for long. A departed being able to hold a straight razor and use it to cut someone's wrists was very unlikely.

Could it have been a reflection off a television or a computer? Absolutely. A tablet? Yes, to all three. But what were the odds Halle would have slit wrists while a movie played in the background that just happened to have a man holding a straight razor?

I pulled into the marina and found the slip Halle was temporarily renting. According to Jason, she usually moored off her father's property, but the dock had been damaged in a recent storm so she'd had to move to the marina while Donald had it repaired.

The houseboat, a gorgeous single-story that probably cost more than my life, barely fit into the slip. All the lights were out save a night-light in the kitchen. I stepped onto the boat and knocked on the door off a small outdoor patio, but Halle didn't answer. Of course, she didn't. Only rock stars and burglars were awake at this time of night.

I started to leave when the cloth panel on the door moved aside, and a pale face peered out at me.

"Wh–what are you doing here?" she asked, her gaze sliding past me. Checking to see if I'd brought a friend?

I shrugged. "I owe you, and I pay my debts."

"What?" She seemed to panic, which confused me. Though in her defense, confusing me wasn't that hard to do. "You don't owe me anything." Her frantic gaze darted around like a hummingbird caught in a glass jar. When she finished scanning the exterior, she looked over each of her slender shoulders then back again.

Had I caught her with someone? "Look, if you have company…"

"What? No." She straightened, unlocked the door, and cracked it open. "I don't have company. I just don't understand why you're here. In the middle of the night."

"And here I thought we were besties."

"Not without pizza, we aren't."

I laughed. "I'll remember that next time."

She opened the door wider and gestured me inside. "Please, do."

Her place was cool. Modern yet chic. Lots of blues and grays with wood floors and stainless fixtures. But the most appealing aspect of the whole setup was her tiny, moss green terrycloth robe that stopped mid-thigh. And her legs were no joke. Slender, shapely and lightly tinted by the sun.

She closed the door and leaned back against it. "When you say you owe me…?"

"I'm here to see if something's haunting you."

"I was afraid of that."

I leaned a hip against a granite countertop. "You keep fighting me on this. Is there a reason?"

"No," she said, seeming offended. "It's just…I mean, I wouldn't fight you if you really can talk to ghosts."

"We're back to *if*?"

"Oh-em-gee," Aunt Lil said, twirling in the middle of Halle's small kitchen, her floral tent ballooning around her. "I'm moving in."

I crossed my arms over my chest. "She already has a ghost, Aunt Lil. She doesn't need another one."

"But this place is amazing."

"Aunt Lillian is here?" Halle asked, and I grinned at the familial address.

"She is." I glanced around casually but didn't see any other departed. "Would you like me to look for your ghost?"

"Oh, gosh," Halle said, waving a dismissive hand. "I don't want to put you out. You've done so much for me already." She opened the door again, walked over to me, and started pushing me toward it.

"Like what?" I asked, confused again. Maybe my subdural hematoma was flaring up.

She stopped. "Well, you…you…got a blanket for me from that technician, who was in love with you."

"In love?"

"You know what I mean. Crushing on you." She shoved again, inching me toward the door.

"I'm beginning to think you don't want me to find your ghost."

She snorted and slapped my shoulder. "What?"

Why wouldn't she want me to confront the ghost who had supposedly been terrorizing her to the point of making her contemplate suicide for years? Unless…

I gazed down at her as she shoved a hip against my thigh for leverage.

Unless there never was a ghost.

I faced her and took her shoulders. "Halle, what's going on?"

"Nothing." She squirmed out of my grasp. "What do you mean?"

"Was there ever really a ghost? Did you make it all up?"

The shock and indignation that thinned the fullness of her mouth, jutted out her chin, and stiffened every muscle in her body, made me rethink the conclusion I'd haphazardly jumped to. Tears welled in her eyes, and she swallowed hard before saying under her breath, "Please, leave."

"Not until you tell me what's going on."

She turned and grabbed her phone off the counter. "Fine, I'll call the police."

"Fine." I sat on a sofa that lined the front of the living space.

Aunt Lil sat beside me. "Constantine, what's going on? Why are you treating her this way?"

I gave the woman my full attention. "Because she's lying, and I want to know why."

"Yes," Halle said into the phone. "Can you send someone immediately? I have an intruder." She nodded. "The marina. Yes, slip six." She nodded some more, those acting skills coming in handy once again. "You're five minutes away? That's perfect."

She hung up, her expression smug. "You should probably leave before they get here."

With a resigned sigh, I slapped my palms on my knees, winced at the pain that shot all the way down to my ankles, and stood. The elation that flashed across her face convinced me even more that she was hiding something.

I turned toward the door to give her one last shred of hope before ripping it away. "I probably would've left," I said, gesturing toward her phone, "if your volume hadn't been so high."

"What does that mean?"

I leaned closer and whispered, "It means you were listening to the weather report. Not talking to the cops."

Aunt Lil nodded. "Cloudy with a thirty-percent chance of rain."

Having caught Halle red-handed, Aunt Lil and I fist-bumped. Kind of.

Halle slammed her lids shut, took three deep breaths, then refocused on me. "Fine," she said, her serene demeanor reminding me of the calm before the storm. "Do whatever you want. Ask him whatever you want."

"Him?"

Aunt Lil narrowed her eyes. "I feel like there's more to this story than she's letting on."

"But let me just say," Halle continued, "ghosts were humans once, too. And humans, *all* humans, lie."

Aunt Lil gasped. "Did she just call me a liar to my face?"

"No, Aunt Lil. I don't think she's talking to you."

"Well?" Halle asked, tapping an impatient foot on the floor. A bare, impatient foot with ankles and calves as graceful as a swan's neck. She opened her arms to our surroundings. "Do you see anything?"

"You mean like a ghost?"

Her lids slammed shut again, and her fingers curled into fists at her sides as though bracing for the worst. "Yes. Do you see him?"

Back to *him* again.

"Is he talking to you?"

"The ghost?"

"Yes, the ghost!" she said, keeping her eyes squeezed shut, her temper finally uncorking. This was the Halle I knew and loved—the one with the hairpin trigger.

"I don't see anyone but you."

She opened her eyes slowly, one lid at a time, and glanced around. A dawning registered on her face and set her jaw. "Then you're a fraud."

"Am I?" I took a seat again. "I thought we were past this phase."

"Either that or, I don't know. Maybe he's out."

"Out? Out where? Working the night shift at 7-Eleven?"

She whirled around. Looking for the departed? "You said ghosts are always popping in and vanishing when you least expect it. Maybe he's in the vanished stage. Which is too bad, really." The relief that visibly washed over her was hard to miss. "I guess you should go then. No telling how long he'll be gone. Thanks for stopping by, though." She walked to the door and held it open, her brows raised in expectation.

"All right." I stood and stretched but instantly regretted it as pain shot down my side. It was worth it, though, to watch the hope gather in her eyes and shimmer like stardust. "I'll leave." I paused for dramatic effect before adding, "As soon as you tell me why you think it's a man."

"What?" she asked, taken aback.

"Why do you think your ghost is male?"

"Oh, that," she hedged. "I just figured most ghosts are male."

"They aren't."

"Right. Well, I saw him once."

One of my brows, the more sophisticated one, rose in surprise. "Did you?"

"Yes. I forgot to tell you."

"But you don't see ghosts."

"True, but he's been with me a long time. I was bound to see him eventually, right?"

I walked over to the counter, crossed my arms over my chest, and parked a hip there, studying every expression and emotion that flickered across her face. "But how could you see him if you don't normally see the departed?"

She let out a sound that was part frustrated sigh and part growl. I liked it. "How should I know? It's just what people do. Sometimes, they see an apparition, but most of the time, they live their lives completely oblivious to such things. Right?"

"Why?"

"Oh, my God." She whirled away from me while I fought a grin tooth and nail. "I don't make the rules," she continued. "I have Netflix. I know how this stuff works."

I tilted my head in doubt. "I don't know that you do."

She turned back for the sole purpose of setting my face on fire with the heat of her glare.

"Look," I said, letting her off the hook, "if there really is a departed attached to you, it would be attached to you. Like it would never leave your side."

"But Aunt Lillian," she argued.

"Isn't attached to me. She just likes my ass."

"Constantine," Aunt Lil admonished. Then she leaned toward me and giggled. "I mean, you're not wrong."

"And if a departed attached itself to an object you have," I continued, "it would stick to whatever it is like Gorilla Glue."

"Oh, that's good stuff," Aunt Lil said.

"Can the departed pop in and out? Yes, but not with the kind of constant haunting you've been experiencing for years. This is something else." Something I'd been racking my brain to figure out.

She sank onto the sofa and looked as if she were staring through the walls of the houseboat into another time. "But it has to be a ghost. I've seen him."

I fought the urge to go to her. "What did you see? Exactly."

"A ghost walking through my house."

"This house?"

"Yes. No. Every house. He's followed me to every house I've ever lived in. He was even at the hospital when my parents…when they admitted me for observation." The gaze that met mine was so full of anguish and desperation that it leached the breath from my lungs. "He's followed me everywhere for seventeen years. Ever since…" She stopped, her eyes widening before she slammed her mouth shut as if she'd said too much. Her gaze darted to me, scrutinizing my reaction as though wondering if I'd caught on.

I did. "Ever since?" I prodded.

She lifted her chin, preparing to lie. It was her tell.

I held up a hand to stop her. "Never mind. I'll find out for myself." I stood and walked out, much to her surprise. I needed more info, and I was pretty sure I knew where to find it.

Chapter Five

"I'm gonna wing it."
—Me about something I most definitely should not wing.

Half an hour after leaving Halle's place, I was knocking on the door of a lakefront mansion I might've been able to afford if I sold my soul. And my internal organs. And my Harley. No way was I selling my Harley.

A man in his late fifties wearing a T-shirt and a thin pair of sweats answered. I'd felt underdressed until I saw him. Thanks to a late-night text from Jason, he knew I was coming.

"Mr. Nordstrom," I said, greeting him with a nod.

He took my hand in a firm shake. A businessman, through and through. "Mr. Vause, call me Donald."

"And please call me Eric."

He gestured me inside. "I have it set up in my office, but if you have any questions—"

"I have several thousand."

He pressed his lips together and nodded. "I thought you might." He led me down a long hallway with wooden floors to his home office.

"Sorry for the late-night visit."

"Please, don't apologize." He shook his head and rubbed his red-rimmed eyes with a thumb and index finger. He'd been crying. Jason must've told him about the fate I'd seen for his daughter. "Anything I can do," he said, his voice cracking. "Any time, day or night."

"Thank you."

He sat me behind a massive oak desk and woke up his computer. A video was already cued up. "Just press play."

I viewed the grainy video from a surveillance camera set up in Halle's kitchen on the houseboat. The angle captured a tiny bit of her bedroom as she slept in the background. I could only see her blond head given the covers she had pulled up to her chin.

After a moment, a dining room chair slid slowly across the kitchen floor, scraping the tile and not stopping until it butted up against a cabinet. Creepy? Yes. Legitimate? That remained to be seen.

The video flickered as the timestamp jumped forward, the clips pieced together rather shoddily. The next clip showed a cup launching itself off the countertop and crashing against the fridge. The clip had sound, and the crash was loud enough to wake the dead. Metaphorically. But Halle didn't move. Didn't even flinch. That fact was even more suspicious than the cup.

"There's one more event," Donald said.

I waited until the next flicker. This clip was from the same camera, only this time, I saw Halle's face in the background, blurry and monochromatic but clearly her. She breathed softly with her hands under her chin, which didn't change, even when the blanket covering her slid down to reveal her complete state of undress.

Though I should have looked away, I didn't blink until the door to her bedroom slammed shut with a violent boom that would've shaken the whole boat. It was almost a warning to anyone watching—a very possessive one.

"That's it," Donald said. He'd walked away to gaze out a huge plate glass window, unable to watch what his daughter had been going through.

The timestamp between the three clips showed they'd happened only a few minutes apart, and if not for a few minor points, I might've bought the whole thing. But probably not. I'd been at this for a long time.

"What do you think?" he asked.

"How old is this?"

"About a year. It was captured right before Halle's mother died."

"Jason said you had it checked out?"

"Yes. Our head of security says it's legit. He also investigated her houseboat. There was no evidence of tampering. Nothing tied to the chair or the cup."

"And Halle didn't see anyone when she woke up?"

"That's just it. She didn't. She slept through the whole thing. It was actually our head of security who noticed it a few days later and brought it to our attention." He pointed at the computer screen as though accusing it of wrongdoing. "We had her committed because of all this, Eric." His voice broke, and he had to step away to gather himself. He gazed out of the window again, the darkness beyond impossible to penetrate save for a few flickers of moonlight glistening on the waves across the lake. "Years ago, we had her institutionalized because we thought she was delusional. And then we saw this video."

The guilt was clearly eating him alive.

"And now you think she's going to be murdered?" A husky sob rushed out of him, and he fought to keep his emotions under control.

I gave him a moment before asking, "Can you email this to me?"

"Of course. But you haven't told me what you think."

"I don't have an opinion just yet," I lied. "But let me ask you, in all of the years you've had security cameras on Halle, is this the only video showing any supernatural events?" And three in one night, too. How convenient.

"My wife and I tried for years to figure this out. To come up with a reason for what we thought were Halle's delusions. To figure out exactly when it all started."

"And?"

He shook his head. "We never came up with a specific time, place, or incident. One day, we just noticed that she was, I don't know how to say it…"

"As honestly as you can."

"That she was going downhill." He raked a hand through his thinning hair. "Or maybe she'd already hit rock bottom by the time we caught on. She's a very good actress."

"I noticed."

"She didn't confide in us for years. Then one day, out of the blue, she told us she was being haunted. That a ghost had been following her, of all things. We thought she was joking at first, but the more time that passed, the further into depression she sank, and we realized she believed, truly believed, she was cursed."

I bent my head in thought. "How old was she?"

"When she told us? Fifteen."

"But her behavior had already changed before that?"

He nodded. "Looking back, I'd say she'd been depressed for at least two years before that. Maybe three."

"Years?" I asked, my astonishment—my prejudice—shining through.

"I know." He rubbed his forehead and sank into a leather chair across from me. "Like I said, either she hid it really well, or we were oblivious. I never thought we were bad parents until I saw that video. It changed everything. It's not that we didn't support her, but we never believed her.

And now I know that was even worse."

Part of me wanted to sympathize with him. With his plight. But to miss something so detrimental… It hit closer to home than I wanted to admit.

Then again, this wasn't about me. It was about Halle and how we were going to perform a miracle. How we could change her fate.

I considered the video again as Donald spoke.

"I know she seems fine," he said to me, "but don't let her fool you. Ever since Emma died last year, Halle has gone into a tailspin. She puts on a brave face, but when she comes to work with dark circles under her eyes, hands shaking, and fingernails chewed to the quick… I'm at my wit's end, Eric. I just don't know what else to do. And now this?" He buried his face in his hands, and a sob shook his shoulders.

"May I ask how your wife died?"

"Car accident. A horrible car accident. She overshot a curve in the mountains and… There was little left of her or the vehicle."

My instincts kicked in so hard they almost knocked me unconscious, especially with the knowledge of what awaited Halle. "Was there anything unusual about the accident?"

He blew his nose into a tissue and looked at me in surprise. "The whole damned thing was unusual."

"Like?"

"She had no reason to be on that road, first of all. And a mechanic speculated that her brakes failed, but we'd just had maintenance done. Those brakes were pristine."

I had an inkling I knew what was going on, but I needed a segue that wouldn't look suspicious. I came up with one and crossed my fingers. "You said your head of security checked out Halle's houseboat after this happened?"

"Yes."

"I'd like to talk to him, see if he remembers anything out of the ordinary from that night."

"I'll get you his information." He took out his phone to look it up.

I cleared my throat and asked as nonchalantly as I could, "Did he install her security system?"

"Yes," he said absently while scrolling through his contacts. "My company has used him for years, and he also takes care of our home security."

I typed my next question into my phone, cleared my throat again to get his attention, and turned it to show him my screen.

He furrowed his brows, read my message, and started to answer. If I hadn't slammed an index finger over my mouth to shush him, he would've done just that. I pointed to his phone to clue him in.

After a moment of contemplation, he opened a notes app, typed his answer, and turned his cell to show me.

Seventeen years. Their security guy had worked for his company for seventeen years. I'd recently heard that exact number from a Nordstrom much prettier than Donald.

"So, Jason tells me you have a killer wine cellar." He didn't, but Donald was rich. All rich people had wine cellars, and they were all killer.

When I nodded at Donald, encouraging him to play along, he nodded back. "I do. Would you like to see it?"

"I thought you'd never ask."

He unfolded himself from the chair, but before he could lead the way, I took his phone out of his hands and put it alongside mine on his desk. I reassured him with yet another nod, and he led me through the house, down a narrow set of stairs, and into a dimly lit basement. The walls were made of stone, with row after row of wine bottles and a huge walk-in cooler.

Sure enough, one killer wine cellar, as ordered. And the walk-in cooler was like a birthday present I never saw coming.

I pulled the massive steel door open and gestured for Donald to follow me. Once the door closed, I lowered my voice and asked him, "There aren't any cameras in here, right?"

He shook his head.

After scanning the area to double-check, I turned back. "We can't be certain it's not bugged, but I would be surprised if it were."

"Bugged?" he asked.

"Let's keep our voices as low as possible, just in case."

"I don't understand."

"Before we get to that," I said, speaking as softly as I could, "the video you showed me is about as fake as my membership card to the Yacht Club."

He took a long moment to study me, size me up, and decide if he should believe anything coming out of my mouth. If we hadn't been able to save Zachary's life today, I think he would've kicked me out on my ear. But that, along with Jason's endorsement, was enough to keep his skepticism at bay. For the moment. "How do you know?"

"First, every event was perfectly framed. Nothing happened out of the camera's field of view. Almost as if it were staged."

He seemed to think back and then agreed with a nod.

"Second, Halle never woke up. She never flinched. Her breathing never wavered."

"W–wait," he said, struggling to form the words he didn't want to speak. "Do you think Halle was drugged?"

"I do. And third, there were no departed in the room."

He shook his head, trying to process everything I was saying. "How can you know that?"

"My ability allows me to see the departed on film, in digital recordings, Polaroids, pretty much anything. They look just like everyone else to me, only a little blurrier, and the colors aren't quite as vibrant. But who knows? My new reality defies the laws of physics and rarely makes sense. Especially to me. Maybe different kinds of recordings—"

"No. No, I think you're right."

"Why?"

"It was just strange how he came to us with the so-called evidence. I mean, why was he looking at recordings of her in the first place? They were there only if we needed to review something."

I could tell his mind was racing, connecting the dots as they appeared.

"And one reason it took so long for us to believe Halle was that every time she told us a glass broke or a cabinet door slammed, there was nothing on the video to prove it. I slowly began to realize the videos Paul showed us, the ones with nothing on them whatsoever, were the same. Her blender always in the same spot. Her fruit basket always filled with the same fruit."

"Paul is your head of security?"

"Yes. Paul Meacham. But the videos he showed us changed, just when I became suspicious. Different placement. Different fruit. Until, eventually, Halle gave up. She stopped telling us when things happened. She stopped trusting us completely." A sob shook his shoulders again.

"If my instincts are correct, and they always are, your head of security has been terrorizing your daughter for seventeen years."

He pressed a hand to his mouth and stumbled back against a wine rack, the shock weakening his legs. It was about to get worse.

"Donald, I hate to ask this"—and I really did—"but do you think your wife grew suspicious of him?"

He stilled, and the blood drained from his face as he thought back. "No," he whispered, but it was an expression of denial. Simply too much for him to process. "Please, no. Why would he do that? Why would he do any of this?"

"I don't know, but I think Halle does." When he only gaped at me, I explained. "She knows more than she's letting on. I'm not saying she suspects your head of security, but something definitely happened to her seventeen years ago, and we need to find out what it was."

Another sob racked his body, and I let his emotion take over for a few minutes before continuing with my plan.

"How good are your acting skills?"

He sniffed and looked at me like I was crazy. "I've brokered billion-dollar business deals. Denzel wishes he was this good."

I knew I liked him. "Perfect. You can't let on that you suspect anything. Just act natural, whether you're making breakfast or in a business meeting. If you usually sing in the shower, sing in the shower. Don't change your routine. Not until we know more."

"What if I'm going about my business, Paul walks by, and I accidentally stab him forty-seven times?"

"No stabbing him. We don't know that he actually had anything to do with this. And even if he did, we can't prove it. Not yet."

"Fine." I could see the anger welling up inside him, and it would only get worse the more he thought about everything that'd led up to this day. It would bubble and simmer and eventually boil over, and then I wouldn't be able to stop him. I needed to figure this out before that happened.

"We need to keep this between us, obviously. You can fill Jason in with explicit instructions to keep quiet but don't do it over the phone. Don't call or text anything about this and instruct him to do the same. Tell him in a loud and crowded place, far away from your phones. We may need his help."

"Should I do it now?"

"No. It'll look suspicious if you leave in the middle of the night right after I was here."

"Okay." He swallowed hard, bracing himself for the trials to come. "First thing in the morning. But what about my daughter? We have to stop what is going to happen to her."

"That's the plan. You just need to trust me." I didn't mention how ridiculous that statement was. I barely trusted myself, and I was asking this man, a stranger, to place his daughter's life in my hands. Apparently, the old saying was true: Fake it 'til you make it.

Chapter Six

It took me halfway through to realize
my life story has an unreliable narrator.
—True fact

I couldn't tell if the incessant pounding came from the door to my motel room or my head. It was probably the door since it woke up the furry creature at my side. Either way, it was unwelcome and unwanted.

I tried to ignore it, but the visitor was annoyingly polite. Three knocks, just loud enough for me to hear, and then a few seconds of blessed silence before they tried again. Eventually, one of us would give in, and I vowed it would not be me. Until I heard a lyrical voice calling out my name.

My eyes flew open, and I tried to sit up, but pain shot through every molecule of my body. I suddenly remembered why I'd downed half a fifth the night before—well, one reason I'd downed half a fifth the night before. Several different types of pain had set up shop in my extremities. And my intremities, come to think of it. Shooting, stabbing, throbbing, and just plain excruciating. I now had a deep understanding of adjectives I never knew existed.

Just then, I heard the locking mechanisms turn, and the door opened, spilling a harsh and excessively bright stream of sunlight into the room. I squeezed my eyes shut to block it out as Halle hurried over and sat beside me on the edge of the bed. She felt my forehead before sliding her hand to my cheek, then my neck, then my chest. "Eric?"

Lower.

"Are you awake?"

Just a little lower.

A male voice interrupted our moment. "Do I need to call an ambulance?"

"Do it and die," I said, my voice hoarse and unrecognizable.

Halle spoke softly to him. "No. Thank you, Nolan. He had a rough night. Now, he's cranky."

"I don't know. That's a lot of blood."

My leg wound had opened up at some point, but I stopped the bleeding with a little pressure and a lot of cursing.

"And we don't allow dogs."

I had a dog?

"It's okay," Halle said.

Oh, right. The furball.

"I'll take care of it. I'll pay for the sheets and have the mattress and carpet cleaned."

"You don't have to do that," he said, his tone suddenly flirtatious. "The boss doesn't need to know everything, but he should probably check out soon."

"I'll take care of it," she repeated.

I tried to look at her, but I just couldn't focus on anything other than the backs of my eyelids. Either that fifth had hit me harder than usual, or my subdural hematoma was acting up again. Of course, her hand resting on my rib cage wasn't helping. I had focus issues as it was. Her ministrations were only making them worse.

Darkness fell over the room when the man closed the door, and I asked in a gravelly voice, "Who's Nolan?"

"A friend from high school who works here. Who's this?" She picked up the pitch-black furball. It whimpered excitedly in her arms. Halle laughed, the sound curative.

"Her name is Buttercup."

"Does she have a collar with a tag?"

"No, but she reminds me of a hellhound named Buttercup."

"You know a hellhound named Buttercup?"

"She's a cuddler, too."

"Well, this little sweetheart needs her own name. How about Fluffy? Or Flavia? Or Flutura the Warrior Queen?"

The horrified expression I flung at her was more than warranted. "What is wrong with you?"

She hmphed and continued to snuggle the pup, cooing and crooning. I'd never been so jealous of an animal in my life.

I threw an arm over my eyes, realizing I probably looked like death warmed over. The longer the night wore on, the more swelling appeared, and the worse my scrapes, bruises, and the deep abrasion across my jaw got. Then I remembered my arm looked just as bad, so I gave up and went back to admiring the view.

She wore a peach sundress with a pale-yellow sweater like a summer breeze come to life.

"Why aren't you at work?" I asked.

"I was on my way, but I thought I'd stop by and check on you."

"How did you know where to find me?"

"You texted me seventy-three times last night and invited me over."

I bolted upright, ignoring the onslaught of pain as I scrambled for my phone. If I texted anything to her about Paul, the security guy, he would know. No way he didn't have some kind of surveillance on both Halle's and her father's phones. How could I be so careless? And only hours after I'd promised Donald he could trust me with his daughter's life.

"Kidding," she said in a sing-song voice. She buried her face against the furball's neck. "Jason told me. Where did you get Flutura?"

After squelching a burning desire to throttle her, I scooted up on the bed and swung my legs over the side, careful to keep the sheet covering my most pertinent parts. "First, we're not calling her that. And second, she was outside my door last night, whimpering in the rain."

Halle turned the full force of her admiration on me with a single, heart-stopping smile. "And you brought her inside?"

It was admiration I didn't deserve. I ducked my head and checked my phone for messages. "She was shivering."

"And then you let her sleep with you?"

I stopped and stared yet again. "She was shivering."

She stared back. For a really long time. Long enough that my lungs began to burn, and I realized I'd stopped breathing.

While I sat there like an ass, struggling to provide my cells with oxygen, she was apparently more worried about the mutt. "Flavia!" she shouted, shifting her focus back to the tiny creature.

"No." I lurched to my feet, dislodging her when I took the sheet with me.

She squeaked out a protest and jumped up, cradling the pup to her as though its life were in danger.

I wrapped the sheet tighter and stepped around her to get to the bathroom and, more importantly, the shower. But when I passed, I caught a glimpse of her expression in the mirror, the distress that flickered across her face when she scrutinized every visible inch of me. I certainly didn't mind the attention, but the concern was unwarranted.

"It looks worse than it feels," I lied.

Busted, she met my gaze in the mirror and shook her head. "I doubt that."

I paused before disappearing into the bathroom and asked, "You worried about me?"

As though unable to admit it, she pulled the pup closer and headed for the door. "I'm going to take Flo for a walk."

"Flo?"

"Short for Florabel," she said, so matter-of-factly I laughed out loud.

It hurt.

So did washing and shampooing and moving in general. I decided to preserve what energy I could and forego shaving for the time being. The scruff would help disguise the abrasions, too. Win-win.

The shower helped with the soreness, but painkillers were still on the breakfast menu. As for the rest of the day, I needed to get Halle to trust me. To open up. If she knew something about Paul Meacham that would help us figure this out… But what? Had he assaulted her when she was a kid? Was she afraid of him? Her secretive behavior would suggest an absolute yes to both of those questions, but I didn't want to assume anything. And I didn't want to risk her mental well-being.

Unless I absolutely had to.

Halle's signature knock sounded at the door.

I strolled over and asked through said door, "Who is it?"

"It's me."

"Me, who?" Yes, I was a five-year-old trapped inside a thirty-three-year-old's body.

"I got breakfast burritos."

I swung the door open. "Way to bury the lead."

She stood there, food in one arm and the furball in the other, as I walked back to the mirror. I'd been in the middle of trying to tame the mop that grew wild on the top of my head—a testament to the never-ending struggle of man versus nature.

I was brushing my hair with my fingers when our gazes met in the mirror mid-fluff. She was still standing at the door like a deer in headlights. I looked down and realized the massive bruise that ran from my lower left abdomen up to my right shoulder must've surprised her. "It's not as bad as it looks. Promise."

She blinked back to life and stepped inside, closing the door behind her. "I didn't know what you liked, so I got a couple of options."

"Always a good plan. You didn't happen to pick up a bottle of morphine while you were out, did you?"

"No, but I have some ibuprofen."

That'd work. Hopefully.

She put the furball on the bed. It yipped and ran in circles, as excited about the burritos as I was.

I gave up on my hair and sat at the small table by the window as she put a box on the floor and unpacked the bag. I wondered about the box. Not enough to ask, but… She lifted out a cup of coffee. "Coffee, too?" I stole one and took a sip. Lukewarm but mouthwateringly delicious. "You must really like me."

She paused, cast me a sideways glance, then continued her work. "I got one with bacon, one with ham, and one with sausage. And can I just say, for the record, you look really good in a towel?"

I stilled. Was that a compliment? Did she just compliment me? And, fuck, I *was* in a towel.

"I'm sorry." I jumped up, grabbed an armful of clothes, and headed back to the bathroom. "I live in a kind of compound," I said through the door, "with like a thousand other people, and none of us were gifted with an overabundance of manners."

Even when I stepped out in a Cruisers T-shirt and jeans, she continued to avoid eye contact. Fucking hell, I could be an ass. Unless I was greatly mistaken, this woman had been the victim of a malicious criminal for a long time. She'd very likely been assaulted at a young age and then stalked for years, possibly worse. And here I was, walking around half-naked.

I sat again, stretched one leg under the table, and draped an arm over it. She didn't flinch or back away. A good sign. Hopefully, I hadn't scarred her for life.

"I'm really sorry about that."

She shook her head. "No, I'm sorry. I shouldn't have said that. It's just, I've never seen a body like yours in real life. I wasn't sure they really existed."

I frowned and surveyed my body parts. Apart from a few tattoos that were filched from various Asian criminal organizations—and would probably get me killed as a result—the rest of my ink was pretty average American biker. But if someone grew up very sheltered, my inked-up physique could be quite the eye-opener.

"You live in a compound with a thousand people?"

I laughed softly. "No. It just feels like it sometimes. I live in a compound with about twenty other people, but it's not a cult. I swear." I was always worried about our image.

She nodded and gestured toward the spread. "Pick your poison."

"You first."

"Oh, I'm not hungry. You can eat one now and save the others for later. You have a fridge." She pointed to the small apartment fridge beside the dresser.

Her behavior was beginning to worry me. Did my negligence bother her more than she was letting on? Did I trigger some residual PTSD? I needed to figure out a way to make Halle trust me and, so far, my technique sucked.

She poured a tiny pouch of puppy food onto a napkin, set it on the floor, and put the furball in front of it. The pup dove in like she was starving. As if I hadn't just fed her half of a cheeseburger three hours ago.

"How about Florida?"

"I'm game," I said after swallowing another sip. "When do we leave?"

A dimple appeared at one corner of her mouth. "I meant for the puppy."

"That seems like a long way to send her, but okay. Do you think she has family there?"

She giggled. "For her name."

"Ah. You like F-L names, I take it?"

"No more than any other combination. She just seems like an F-L kind of dog."

"Okay, then." Hard to argue with that kind of logic.

"You're not eating," she said with a frown.

"I'm letting the coffee burn a hole in my stomach first. Food always dampens the hallucinogenic properties of caffeine, and I need all the hallucinations I can get."

She forced a fake laugh—tough crowd—and sat across from me. Keeping her gaze downcast, she stuck a nail between her teeth before catching herself and folding her hands in her lap.

Now was my chance, but how much should I tell her? How much *could* I tell her? Then I remembered, not a whole damned lot. Again, her phone was almost surely being monitored. While I didn't know for certain security guy Paul was involved in any of this, I just couldn't risk him, or whoever *was* behind it, overhearing our conversation.

I could ask her to take the day off, ditch our phones, and head somewhere isolated. She worked for her father, after all. Surely, she could get away with playing hooky for one day. The trick would be to explain why we were ditching our phones and going to an isolated area without tipping off my number-one suspect, and putting her, or anyone else, in even more danger.

"Can I ask you something?" she said, dragging me out of my thoughts.

"Okay, but I think it really was to get to the other side."

"I was wondering, and you can absolutely say no," she qualified, showing me her palms as proof, "but I was wondering if you would like to have sex with me."

She could have slapped me with a flyswatter, and I would've been less stunned. I sat there gaping at her like a fool as she chewed on a nail.

She dropped her hand and continued. "It's just…I've never met anyone like you." Her gaze traveled the length of my mutilated body. "I've never seen anyone so beautiful in my life. I didn't know people like you existed outside of magazines."

Clearly, she'd never looked in a mirror.

"And I've never met anyone who can do the things you can."

She needed to get out more.

"Not to mention the fact that you're a good person."

I felt the need to stop her right there. "Why? Because I brought a puppy in from the cold?"

"And you saved Zachary."

"I saved Zachary because I didn't want that on my conscience for the rest of my life. That doesn't make me a good person. It makes me selfish and self-absorbed."

"Ah. Well, that explains everything, but there's more."

"Yeah?"

She drew in a deep breath—I got the feeling it was for courage—and let the words leave her mouth as fast as her tongue would carry them. "I've never wanted anything more in my life than I want your body."

And that was my undoing. At first, she'd shaken me so hard I couldn't move. But it didn't take long for my baser instincts to kick in. I started forward, only to find out she wasn't finished, and her next words would flip my world off its axis.

"Besides a Malibu Barbie Dreamhouse, but I was seven. And I just figured I'd take a chance, I'd quit being a wet noodle and ask for what I want for the first time in my life since, as you know,"—her gaze met mine at last—"I'm going to be dead in two months."

Chapter Seven

I'd date me.
Mainly because I put out.
—Meme

As if she hadn't shaken me enough. As if she hadn't upended my world and sent me spiraling, she had to throw her impending doom into the mix. I sat dumbfounded, unsure of what to do. What to say.

"Halle," I began, but she cut me off.

"It's okay. I knew it was coming."

Words wouldn't form in my mouth. Not that I knew what to say if they would. I tried to see into her mind, to figure out what she was thinking, but I wasn't that kind of psychic. "How?" I asked at last. It was all I could get out.

"How did I know it was coming, or how do I know it's coming in precisely two months?"

"Either," I said, flustered. "Both."

"I don't know. Something has changed. The apparition is getting more aggressive. Angrier."

"How do you know?"

"Just everything that happens."

"Like what?"

"I don't know," she said, clearly growing frustrated with my questions. "Just usual ghost stuff."

"Like what?" I repeated.

She released an annoyed sigh. "Mostly cabinet doors slamming shut. Objects moving in the night. Water overrunning the sink. The usual. But sometimes..." She chewed on a nail before finishing her statement. "Sometimes, I wake up naked with no memory of taking off my clothes."

A sharp, simmering rage settled deep in the pit of my stomach. Now I knew for certain none of this was supernatural in nature. Not that I needed additional proof, but it was nice to have backup. The departed didn't drug people and then strip them in the middle of the night. Sick, deranged stalkers did.

Her cheeks flushed a bright pink. She was embarrassed, and that made me even angrier. "Nothing ever happens. It's not like I'm being assaulted or anything."

I wondered how she could be so sure. "Assault comes in many forms."

She hugged herself and shook her head, unable to even contemplate such a violation.

"When you were upset at the gas pump, you said it was because you got an alert that your house was on fire," I said, changing the subject.

"Yes, but it wasn't. I get alerts all the time, and they are only true about half the time."

Because Meacham was toying with her. Sending her on wild goose chase after wild goose chase. Wearing her down in preparation for her staged suicide. "How is he getting more aggressive?"

"He's been leaving death threats."

"Death threats?" That was new. "What kind?"

"Notes. Sometimes, on a fogged window. Other times, in spilled sugar. Just wherever he can."

"Your father didn't say anything about that."

"You spoke to my father?" When I nodded, she shrugged a timid shoulder. "I haven't told him."

"Why not?" I asked, appalled.

"I can't put my dad through any more. This has taken over his whole life. And with my mom's death? I just can't."

"What do the notes say?"

She pulled her lower lip between her teeth, stalling. She stalled some more when she said, "I can't always read them."

"Halle," I warned.

Her shoulders deflated as she released a surrendering sigh. "At first, they were just numbers. They started right after my mom died. The number twelve kept popping up. But a month later, it changed to an eleven. Then a ten. Then a nine."

"A countdown."

"Yes. Every month for the last year, he's been counting down. And now we're at number two." She leveled an accusing gaze on me. "And you've known since the first time you laid eyes on me."

"Not the first time," I said, slightly offended. "What makes you think they're death threats? They could mean anything."

"Because the other note he leaves is pretty explicit. It's just one word. *Payback*."

Ah. Now we were getting somewhere. "Halle, what happened seventeen years ago? What changed your life so dramatically? And who wants payback?"

She shook her head and looked away, tears shimmering in her eyes.

I leaned onto my elbows and put a hand over hers. "Halle, I know this is hard, but please trust me."

"It's not that. It's not that I don't trust you. You've earned that and then some. But if I tell you what happened, what I did, you won't want to have sex with me anymore."

I almost snorted. Clearly, she didn't understand the male thought process.

But I needed to chill. I was pushing her too hard. I wanted her to bend. Not break.

The furball started whimpering at her feet. Halle picked her up, nuzzled her, then set her in the box she'd brought along with a dry towel from the bathroom. With a full belly, the furball settled immediately and went to sleep.

Halle straightened and walked over to stand in front of me. "Is that a yes?"

"No," I said, taking in every curve she had to offer. She smelled sweet, like jasmine. "It's a hell yes." I put a hand on her hip, the heat from her body soaking into my skin as she straddled me.

With hesitant fingers, she tested the abrasion on my jaw. "Are you sure this is okay? You were hit by a truck yesterday."

"I was sideswiped by a truck. Huge difference."

She nodded and grew thoughtful as though making calculations in her head. Now was not the time for math.

"I'm pretty sure you're a supernatural being," she said, completely serious. "That you're not real and will disappear as soon as all of this is over."

"I have several friends who are supernaturally inclined. I am not one of them. And I'm not going anywhere."

She buried her fingers in my hair and covered my mouth with hers. I'd never welcomed a kiss more in my life. My pants tightened as she sank farther onto my lap. She tasted like cherries and Sprite.

She broke the kiss without warning and looked down at me, her brows drawn. "You have to tell me if I hurt you."

"That's my line."

"Pinkie swear?" She presented her pinkie for me to swear on, and I tried not to laugh.

After wrapping my pinkie around hers, she nodded and asked, "Okay, what's next?"

"What?" I asked, taken aback.

"Well, we kissed, and…I mean, I know what's next." She laughed at herself and waved a dismissive hand. "Kind of. I've just never actually done it."

"Holy fuck." I lifted her off me and set her on the bed like she was contagious.

She fell back, the skirt of her dress flying over her head. It was a nice image, but…

"Are you…?" I couldn't even say the words—not out loud. So, I whispered, "Are you a virgin?"

She patted her dress down and looked up at me. "Technically, yes."

I stood motionless for a solid minute before raking my hands through my hair and pacing. "This isn't possible."

"Why?" she asked, suddenly self-conscious, incessantly smoothing her dress as though the act were a coping mechanism.

"No," I said with a breathy laugh. I shook an index finger. "No one who looks like you is a virgin at… Wait, how old are you?"

"I'm twenty-nine, and I'm offended. What does that have to do with anything?" She kept vigil with a chastising scowl as I paced back and forth in front of her.

I stopped as realization dawned. "Wait, is this a I-don't-want-to-die-a-virgin thing?"

"No." She stood and started gathering her belongings. "How shallow do you think I am?"

"Then what is it?"

She faced me, her neck and cheeks a brilliant pink. I almost felt guilty for my reaction. Almost. "This is a you-are-the-most-beautiful-thing-I've-ever-seen-in-my-life-and-I-want-to-lick-every-inch-of-your-body thing."

Holy shit, she was direct. After taking a moment to process, I let a grin lift one corner of my mouth. "Why didn't you say so?"

The glare she fired at me like a scud missile suggested she was not amused. "I believe I did." Her blue eyes shimmered with unspent tears, twisting a knot inside my heart. "I said things out loud to you that I've never said to anyone. And you're upset that I'm technically a virgin?"

"I'm sorry." I pulled her into my arms and rested my chin on the top of her head, but she remained stiff, refusing to yield. I'd have to work hard to make reparations. I'd have to… "Wait." I set her at arm's length. "Why are you only technically a virgin?"

Her chin lifted in defiance. "I messed around with Peter Scarsdale in ninth grade. We got to second base."

I didn't know whether to laugh or laugh really hard. I didn't want to offend her any more than I already had. How had this stunning creature remained untouched for almost thirty years? Then it hit me. The incident. Whatever had happened to her must've scarred her worse than anyone realized. I pulled her stiff body into my arms again. I would have to tread carefully. Take this slow. Proceed at a snail's pace.

"Can we have sex now or not?"

I coughed into a closed fist to disguise a burst of laughter I couldn't have stopped if I'd tried. My life had gotten so weird after that hell demon possessed me, and then this angel showed up and flipped everything upside down. We would figure out how to cheat death. How to stop fate. And the first step was putting Paul Meacham behind bars.

Actually… I set her at arm's length again. The first step was seeing to this exquisite being who had a few supernatural powers herself. Namely, dissolving men's bones with a single glance.

I lifted her chin, her blue eyes shimmering in the sunlight, and pressed my mouth to hers. She remained as stiff as the suspension on a Harley-Davidson hardtail until I slid my tongue between her lips and dove deep inside her. She melted against me and even went so far as to grab handfuls of my T-shirt for stability.

After walking her back to the bed, I eased her onto it and sank to my knees in front of her. She wrapped her arms around my neck and tightened her hold when I tried to pull back. I let her take the lead for a moment as she explored my mouth, at first hesitantly and then with more fervor, tilting her head and pushing her tongue against mine. Her fingers found their way into my hair and held me still as she tried various techniques, almost as though she'd been studying up and wanted to experience them all. Which, oddly enough, worked for me.

While she practiced mouth-to-mouth, I went to work on the chest compressions. I unbuttoned the top of her dress and thanked the gods for front-clasp bras. I unhooked it and watched as two gorgeous orbs spilled out. And I thought she couldn't be any more perfect.

When I brushed a thumb over one nipple, she gasped from behind the kiss, pulling in cool air between our lips. When I broke away to run my tongue over that same dusky peak, she cradled my head to her chest, her breaths coming in quicker and quicker succession. When I slid a hand under her dress and up her thigh, she parted her legs and eased forward on the bed until my fingers found soft curls.

Which meant she wasn't wearing panties. I had to pause and take a moment as blood flooded my erection, hardening me even further. It had been a while. I almost came in my pants when I felt the slickness and warmth of her folds.

I held her to me and put my mouth at her ear. "I'm going to make you come, okay?"

"But you're going to join me, right?" she asked, her voice breathy.

I shook my head. I couldn't. Not until I knew what'd happened to her. I didn't want to trigger any bad memories, and she didn't need a rutting stag taking advantage of her. "Next time."

She leaned back and frowned. "But I want to lick you."

A grin spread so far across my face it hurt my abrased jaw. "You can lick me next time."

She made a whimpering sound of protest, which quickly turned into a moan as my fingers slid inside her. She tightened around them, and I had to take deep, purposeful breaths just to keep the possibility of spontaneous ejaculation at bay.

"Are you okay?" I asked before proceeding.

She breathed out one word that reflected her personality to a flawless degree. "Exceedingly."

That'd do. I hooked an arm under one knee and slid down her body, kissing her inner thighs until I reached her perfect center. I slid my tongue along the silky folds and then brushed it across her swollen clit.

She squirmed and strengthened her hold on my hair as if it were the only thing keeping her on this earthly plane.

I pushed my fingers deeper inside and suckled her clit, circling my tongue slowly at first and then with more speed. She grabbed the bedspread on either side of her and stilled, her breath suspended as her muscles tightened around my fingers, pulling them even deeper.

The orgasm hit her hard. She arched her back, her body seizing until she cried out, until she drove her fingers into my hair again and bucked in unison with each trembling ripple as the orgasm pulsed through her, creating exquisite wave after exquisite wave.

I eased onto the bed next to her. She returned to earth slowly, her chest rising and falling as she stared at the ceiling.

"Are you okay, sweetheart?" I asked, a little concerned.

"Why on God's green Earth was I still a virgin? Why did I wait so long?" Her astonished expression had me crying on the inside. "I had no idea."

I raised onto an elbow. "Wait, are you telling me you've never had an orgasm?"

"Is that bad? Is there something wrong with me?"

"No. I'm just surprised. I mean, you've never even…" I let my voice trail off.

She mirrored my position and rested her head in her hand. "You forget, I've had a ghost watching my every move since I was twelve."

One more clue. She'd been twelve when it all started. What'd happened to make her believe she was being haunted so deeply? What'd happened to make her neglect herself and her life so much? "Is that why you're still a virgin?"

She dropped her gaze to a loose thread on the garishly patterned bedspread. "Let's just say, there's a reason Peter Scarsdale only got to second base."

I sat up in alarm. "Halle, what happened?"

"It's silly."

"Tell me."

She pulled at the thread as she spoke. "We were in our basement, watching a movie, and we, you know, started kissing."

"Okay."

"And he started feeling me up."

"Okay." I wasn't actually sure what constituted second base, but it sounded legit.

"And I started feeling him up."

"Gotcha."

"And then it happened."

"What happened?" I asked softly.

"The man. The ghost made his presence known."

"How?"

"The usual. Flashing lights. Volume blaring. Banging sounds."

It would seem Paul Meacham got jealous. Fucking perve.

"Peter freaked and ran out of the house, leaving me in the basement alone. He called me later and asked me what happened, and I made the mistake of telling him."

"You told him you were being haunted?"

"Yes. I thought… I thought he cared about me. The next day, he told everyone at school, and I became a laughingstock. Even though he was scared shitless at the time, he made sure everyone knew I was crazy." She raised her chin, and I fought the urge to kiss it. "I learned my lesson. I never told anyone again—not until my parents a few months later. So, did I ruin the mood?" she asked, biting her lip, the action so provocative I licked my lips in response.

"You want more?" I asked, impressed.

"I want you."

I eased away from her. "Halle, you've been through so much."

She sat up, too. "I get it. I really do. You don't want to hurt me because I still have my V-card."

"That's part of it, yes."

"And you think I'm too fragile to go all the way."

"It's crossed my mind. I just don't think you need anyone taking advantage of you right now. Especially a horny biker with a record."

"So, you don't get to come? Because I gotta tell you, that's the most amazing thing I've ever felt."

"I'm glad you enjoyed it," I deflected. "I'll be here all week."

She emitted a husky laugh, lowered her head, and gazed up at me from underneath her lashes. "But I still want to lick you."

She had a serious oral fixation. Honestly, it was like she was made for me.

"And I want to make you come."

My insides bucked at her bold confession. "You don't have to. I'll live."

"Do I need to give the definition of want? I *want* to give you an orgasm."

"You know how?" I asked, the question a clear challenge.

"I told you, I have Netflix."

"They show that shit on Netflix?"

"Well, it's more implied, but I think I get the gist of it. And you can tell me what I'm doing wrong."

"So, this is like a lesson."

"More like a hands-on workshop." She reached out and ran said hand along the outline of my erection, causing a spike of pleasure that surprised me with how powerful it was.

I covered her hand with mine and squeezed. "Are you sure about this?"

She offered me a smile that was part kitten and part jaguar as she rolled onto her knees and crawled between mine. It was my turn to look up at her. Her clear blue eyes. Her ripe mouth. Her delicate, defiant chin. She bent her head and kissed me long and hard before sliding her hands to the button of my jeans and unfastening them. She slid the zipper down, slipped her hand inside, and encircled my erection with her fingers.

I hissed in a sharp breath as blood surged under her touch.

"Am I doing this right?" she asked, teasing me with a spectacular pout. When I only nodded, she pushed my jeans over my hips and shoved me against the headboard. She did the pouty thing again. "Now, tell me if this hurts."

I was so lost in the moment, I had no idea if she was serious or not. But when she bent down and took me into her mouth, I almost exploded right then and there. And, holy hell, she was right. She did get the gist of it.

Blood rushed into my cock like a flood tide, and I spilled a drop into her mouth. A point of fact we didn't talk about. What would happen when I came? Where should I empty myself?

My breaths came in jagged gasps as she tested how much of me she could take into her mouth. She encircled the base of my cock with one hand and cupped my balls with the other, her teeth grazing the underside of my length as she swallowed almost the entirety of me. My muscles spasmed with each plunge, and I was close to orgasm, but we hadn't talked about the inevitable end.

Without breaking contact, I cupped the back of her head with my hand, threw one leg over her, and laid her back on the bed, straddling her head with my cock still in her mouth. I did it so I could control where I came, but she grabbed hold of my hips and pulled me farther inside. I suddenly realized control was the last thing I had a hold of.

Before I could stop her, before I could warn her of coming events, the sharp sting of orgasm swelled in my abdomen and rocketed through my cock. Pleasure burst through me like a dam breaking, and I came, still cupping her head with one hand and bracing myself against the headboard with the other. I groaned as I spilled my seed into her mouth, worried how she would take it, but she kept hold of my hips, refusing to release me, and swallowed every drop.

When the spasms ebbed, she eased her hold, and I fell onto the bed next to her in awe.

"That's it," I said, dazed and confused. And still panting. "I'm subscribing to Netflix immediately."

She laughed out loud. "I may have watched a how-to video this morning."

"This morning?" I asked, surprised.

"This morning."

"You're a really quick study."

Her lashes floated down shyly to fan across her cheeks. "I wanted to be prepared."

I rolled toward her. "Halle, you didn't have to do that."

The smile she laid on me would've melted a lesser man.

It was me. I was a lesser man. She reduced me to a puddle of primordial goo in three seconds flat.

"You have no idea how much I wanted to," she said. "And it was, I don't know… I don't want to sound cheesy."

"Tell me."

"It was strangely empowering."

Her statement surprised me at first until I realized I understood. "I get that. I felt the same going down on you."

A curious smile spread across her face as she gazed at me. "Have you always been this handsome?"

I laughed. "You'd be surprised how often I don't hear that. Have you always been this beautiful?"

"Now it's your turn to be surprised. I've never found anyone I wanted to share this moment with. I'm glad it was you. I wanted to experience this kind of surreal magic at least once before I die."

My chest tightened at the reminder. "I'm going to do everything in my power to keep that from happening."

She frowned at me. "That's not why I did this, Eric. I don't expect anything from you. Dad and I will figure it out. If my death can be avoided, so be it. If not, that's not on you. I don't want you to feel obligated just because you have this gift."

"Gift?" I asked. I'd never seen it as one. Especially since changing fate had proven far more difficult than I ever imagined. Zachary Church was an exception, not the rule.

"You're a gift whether you see that or not. I hope you find happiness wherever you go."

"You sound like you're saying goodbye."

"Not at all. I hope you stay longer, but I don't want you to feel—"

"Obligated."

She nodded. "Exactly."

I had every intention of staying a while and getting to the bottom of Halle's last moment before it happened. I decided to give it one more shot before calling it a day. There was always tomorrow. "Halle, can you tell me what happened when you were twelve? Can you tell me how all of this started?"

She rolled onto her back and stared at the ceiling, but when next she spoke, her words didn't quite register. They didn't fit, like a dissonant note in a favorite song. She yawned as fatigue took over and then said softly, "It all started when I killed a man in the woods."

Chapter Eight

I either give too many shits or no shits at all.
I can't seem to find that middle ground
for moderate shit distribution.
—True fact

"Can you repeat that?" I asked, not sure I'd heard her correctly.

She faced me again. "I've never told anyone. I've never dared. See?" she said with a sparkling grin. "I told you, you're supernatural. Less than twenty-four hours after meeting you, and I'm having sex for the first time and spilling all my secrets."

She was stalling. I waited for her to gather her thoughts and courage. Surely, she didn't mean she'd actually killed a man. It had to be a metaphor for puberty or something.

"When I was twelve, I went to a cousin's birthday party at Baymore Park. She was turning sixteen and invited me to the cookout. I was so excited to hang with her. She was the cool cousin. Very popular. Very enigmatic."

"And you wanted to be just like her."

She shrugged. "I did. But she was also a bit wild. Always in trouble. And most of that trouble revolved around boys." She started rubbing her hands, and I knew this was not going in a good direction.

I took one of her hands in mine and kissed her knuckles. "Take your time, hon."

She nodded and seemed to think back. "She wanted to go for a walk in the woods, but she was grounded. They only let her have the party because they'd already paid for everything. But my aunt and uncle didn't trust her. That was when I realized why she'd invited me to her party when she never gave me the time of day. Not that I blamed her. I was a twelve-year-old geek. She was the homecoming queen. We may as well have lived on different planets."

"I wish I would've known you when you were a geek."

"Oh, you do. I still am. I just hide it better."

"You think?" I asked in doubt.

She punched me, despite the fact that I'd been sideswiped. Zero respect. "Because my cousin promised we'd be together, they let us go. They thought I'd be a good influence on her."

"Had they met you before that day?"

A bubble of laughter escaped her. "Smartass."

"Sorry," I said, not sorry in the least. "Go on."

"We walked deep into the forest to a set of caves I didn't even know existed. A boy came out. No, a man. He was way older than my cousin with a beer in one hand and a bottle of mouthwash in the other." She looked at me and shrugged. "I still don't get that part."

I wasn't about to tell her. I braced myself for what came next.

"Anna told me to stay outside, said she'd just be a minute, and went into a cave with the man. Only she didn't come back out for a long time. I walked around a little, but it was getting dark, so I went inside. There was no one there. I figured she must've come out when I was walking around and headed back without me."

"Are you fucking kidding me? She left you there?"

"It was partly my fault."

"No, Halle, it wasn't."

"I should've stayed put like she said."

I decided not to argue with her. "What happened after that?"

"The sun was setting, and I'd been walking around for hours. I have, like, zero sense of direction. Anyway, a man found me and told me he was part of a search party. Said the whole town was looking for me. I found out later that wasn't true. Worried she'd get into trouble, my cousin told everyone we got into an argument, and I went home. No one was looking for me. My parents didn't even know I was missing."

I pulled her hand to my chest and held it there. "I'm so sorry, Halle."

"Thank you."

"Do you remember what the man looked like?"

She nodded. "He was huge, like a bear, with a long, dark beard, thick glasses, and a baseball cap.

Paul Meacham was a big guy, but that was where the similarities ended. I'd looked him up on the company website last night. But a beard, thick glasses, and a baseball cap were all perfect articles to help obscure an identity.

"The man started playing tricks on me as we walked. He would take sticks and pretend I had bugs on my legs or accidentally fall into me and, well, touch me inappropriately. Then he would laugh like it was all a joke."

An indignant heat erupted as I listened. She was so vulnerable. So innocent. But I had yet to figure out what this had to do with the Nordstroms' head of security. Had he been working for them yet? Or did he go to work for them because of Halle? And what did any of this have to do with him? She knows him. Surely, she would've recognized him from the forest.

"He kept asking if I wanted to stop and rest. I kept saying no. I got a very bad vibe from him and knew pretty quickly I was in trouble."

Smart girl.

"Finally, he pretended to hurt his ankle and insisted we stop, but when we did, he grabbed my arm and tried to push me to the ground." She was visibly shaking now, and a tear slipped past her lashes. "I fought him with everything I had in me. Then I kicked him, and he tripped on a limb. He fell back and hit his head on a boulder." She swiped at her tears, annoyed with herself. "I took off. I ran until it was too dark to go farther, then I saw lights. I walked to a cabin and asked to borrow a phone. My parents picked me up an hour later. They thought I was staying the night with my cousin."

"And you never told them what happened?"

"I never told anyone. I was too ashamed."

"Why?" I asked. "None of that was your fault."

"For being stupid enough to believe my cousin. For being stupid enough to walk away when she told me to stay put. For being stupid enough to believe the man, even though no one else was searching for me. And for killing him." A sob shook her shoulders, and I pulled her into my arms. "I just kept waiting for the cops to knock on my door. For a set of handcuffs to be locked around my wrists. But that never happened. And to this day, part of me is still waiting."

I ran a hand over her hair. "Are you sure he died?"

She swallowed hard and nodded. "There was so much blood. It soaked into the rock and pooled on the ground around him.

"That doesn't mean—"

"Hikers found his body a few months later," she added, knowing where I was going.

"They found him?"

"Yes," she said between hiccups.

Everything was finally making sense. Well, almost everything. "You think he's been haunting you all this time?"

"I know he has. It started right after."

"And you think you deserve to be haunted. You deserve to be arrested. You deserve to die."

"I do."

"You're so wrong, Halle."

She pressed her mouth together, refusing to believe me.

"Wait, how long after?" I asked. "How long between the incident and the strange events at your house?"

"I don't remember. It took me a while to catch on to the fact that I was being haunted."

"If you had to guess."

"Maybe a couple of weeks? A month?"

I nodded in thought. "And how long did it take for his body to be found?"

"A few months. We were way off the beaten path. It's a miracle it was discovered at all."

"Perhaps." Something else made sense to me now. "Is that why you didn't want me looking for your ghost? You didn't want me talking to him? You thought he would tell me what you did?"

She put a hand over her eyes as though doing so would shut out the painful truth. Once again, I wondered how much to tell her. But this was her story, not mine. She'd been lied to and betrayed by her cousin. By her own parents when they had her committed. By the man in charge of her security for years. She deserved to know the truth. To be in on the plan. But how would I tell her without alerting Meacham? He almost certainly had her phone bugged, but he could also have her bag, watch, or her key fob bugged. Deranged psychopaths should never be underestimated.

I grabbed my phone and did a search for the body they'd found. It had happened almost two decades ago, so it took some time to find the right one, but I did begin to wonder about Idaho and all the discovered bodies. Not that New Mexico was any different.

When I finally located a decent article about it, I asked her, "Do you mind if I show you a picture of the man they found? It's from his driver's license."

She shook her head. "Not at all. I've seen it before, a long time ago."

"Okay, if it bothers you, let me know."

The look on her face, the one that suggested I hung the moon and regularly changed its lightbulb, had me questioning her sanity. Again.

"What?" I asked, wary.

"I've never had anyone treat me like this."

"Like a human?"

"Like my story matters. Like it's valid. Like my emotional distress is real and I was never crazy."

"Like a human," I reiterated. I turned my phone and showed her the pic of a man, clean-shaven

"I barely remember his face, but he does look like the man in the woods. Especially if you add a beard."

"They said he'd been missing for seven months when he was found."

"The timing sounds right. Do you think this is a different guy?" she asked, surprised. "How many dead bodies could there be?"

"Bear with me. When is your cousin's birthday?"

"May 4th."

"And the cookout was actually on her birthday?"

"Absolutely. Anna always insisted her birthday party be celebrated on her actual birthday, no matter what day of the week it fell on. She always said it was stupid to celebrate a birthday the weekend before or the weekend after, just because it was inconvenient."

"She sounds like a peach."

Halle snorted then questioned me with an arch of her brows.

I scrolled to the second paragraph. "Halle, this hiker didn't go missing until a month after your cousin's birthday."

"What?" She sat up and took the phone. "That's impossible." She scanned the paragraph. "His family reported him missing when he didn't show up for work on June 9th of that year." She blinked up at me, then looked back at the article. "A month later. How did I miss that?"

I was saying far too much, considering our entire conversation—and other activities—was probably being monitored. If so, Paul Meacham was on to me. He'd know I suspected Halle wasn't being haunted. That she was being stalked. But he wouldn't know I suspected him.

"Are you saying my attacker isn't the one who's been haunting me?"

Now was the time to let her in on my suspicions and plan, but we needed a little more privacy. I reached over her, grabbed her phone, and walked to the microwave.

"What are you doing?" she asked.

I slanted an index finger over my mouth and locked her phone inside. My worry was that there were other bugs. Walking through the hotel room as naked as the day I was born, I grabbed her purse and gave it the same silent treatment, locking it inside the microwave.

Then I picked up the whimpering furball.

"Don't you dare!" she said, jumping up.

I chuckled and rejoined her in bed.

She took the pup from me, cuddled it to her neck, then gazed up at me with those cobalt eyes. "You saw my last moment in the bar the first time you looked, didn't you?" she asked. Nothing about why I'd just put her belongings in the microwave. Just absolute trust.

"I did see it. I'm sorry."

"It's okay. As far as you knew, I was just an unhinged lady who attacked you over a gas pump. I can hardly blame you for holding back. But what about you?"

"Me? I've attacked people over gas pumps, too. We have so much in common."

"No," she said with a giggle. "Can you see your own last moment?"

"Sadly—or thankfully, depending on your point of view—no."

"But mine is for sure two months from now?"

I pulled her closer. "We can change that, Halle. We did it for Zachary."

"I know. I have complete faith in you. But that's not why I seduced you."

"Are you sure you seduced me? Or was this all part of my evil plan?"

"I don't think you have an evil bone in your body. You gonna tell me why my belongings are in a microwave?"

It was time. Would she believe me? Would she believe that she'd never been haunted but *had* been stalked? I drew in a deep breath and started to explain, when her last moment rushed into my head, the vision as clear and powerful as HDTV. Just like with Zachary, it appeared in my mind without even concentrating. It popped up because the time was so close.

I gaped at her as dread and disbelief slid over me like a blanket of dry ice. It caused a temporary state of paralysis. Of doubt and wariness and astounding denial. My throat constricted, and my eyes watered like I'd taken a shot of battery acid.

"Eric?" Halle asked, growing concerned.

We had indeed changed her fate. Changed her last moment. I lifted my wrist and checked my watch. Seven minutes. Halle had seven minutes to live.

Chapter Nine

I wasn't born so much as summoned.
—T-shirt

Halle's new last moment bore little resemblance to the first one. In this one, she lay naked on a tile floor, her arm covered in blood as she reached out, trying to touch the person who lay on the floor beside her.

Me.

I lay dead, shot in the back, probably trying to get her to the bathroom, so something had clued us into the fact we were in trouble. Just past me stood a man. Since Halle was focused on me, only his legs showed in the vision. Dark gray slacks. Spit-shined Oxfords. And the barrel of a semi-automatic assault rifle.

A calmness enveloped me, despite my pulse having gone supersonic. Thanks to the vision, we had the upper hand. I had to use it to our best advantage. I had to think while the adrenaline spike cleared my head. Her last moment changed after I put her phone in the microwave. He'd probably been listening in and realized I'd caught on when the sound flatlined.

Halle didn't move. She cradled the pup and waited, trusting me to fill her in when I could.

My first priority was to get her out of there, but Meacham was outside somewhere with an assault rifle. We couldn't just go out the front door.

I rushed to my bag, tore through it, and tossed her a T-shirt and a pair of sweats. They would swallow her, but her dress could hinder her escape.

She put them on without question as I hopped into a pair of jeans and ran to the bathroom. The window, probably around the size of Meacham's dick, was too small for Halle to get through, and there was no adjoining door.

Fuck. What had clued us in? Why had we been running for the bathroom?

I glanced at Halle again, studied the memory once more, and looked for the slightest clue to help me devise a plan. At the corner of her vision, shards of glass were on the carpet by Meacham's feet. He was going to shoot us through the window. The curtains were drawn, so he couldn't see in, meaning he may have a thermal-imaging scope. But even thermal imaging couldn't see through walls like in the movies. And the first shots he took didn't hit their marks, allowing us to run for the bathroom.

Realization hit me. He'd intentionally shot out the window and then used his scope to find us. This time, we would act first.

I grabbed Halle just as the first shot hit the wall beside my head.

Halle yelped but allowed me to drag her into the bathroom while three more shots penetrated the window and showered plaster around us. I laid her in the tub with the pup in her arms. My only hope was to lure him inside and then disarm him.

I handed her my phone. "Call the cops and stay put, no matter what you hear."

She nodded, her breaths ragged with fear.

I tried to take the pup out of her arms, but she fought me for the first time, shaking her head frantically.

"I'm going to drop her out the window. She'll be safer outside."

She conceded with a hesitant nod and handed her over.

I opened the tiny window and dropped the pup onto the ground. She whimpered, already spoiled by Halle's attention.

"I'm sorry," Halle said when I turned back to her, huge tears swelling in her eyes. "This is all my fault."

I knelt beside her. "No, it's his fault."

She frowned. "Then whose is it, if not mine?"

"Unless I'm greatly mistaken, it's Paul Meacham's."

"Paul?" she asked taken aback. "He's our head of security."

"Yes. And I believe he was the man in the forest. He's been stalking you, toying with you, for seventeen years."

She pressed a hand to her mouth.

I pointed to the phone and said, "Cops," before leaving. I considered lying on the floor and pretending I'd been shot, but knowing that asshole, he'd put a few more in me for good measure. So, I pressed myself against the wall by the door and waited. If he was any good at this, he'd look through the crack after opening the door and check behind it before entering. Here was hoping he sucked.

"He's coming," Aunt Lil said, and I turned to see her cowering beside me, peeking from behind my arm.

"Can you tell me when he gets to the door?"

"You want me to go out there?" she asked, appalled. When I offered her my best grin, she winked at me. "Sure thing, handsome. But maybe you should call for some backup."

"Halle's calling the cops."

"No, I meant some more…aggressive backup."

Somehow, I'd been assigned as hellhound wrangler at the compound. Probably because they all slept with me. But that didn't mean I knew anything about how to control them. "I don't know how to summon them. And even if I could, they're incorporeal."

"For the most part, but they're hellhounds. Have you learned nothing?"

Apparently, not.

"He's at the door," she whispered like he would've heard her had she not.

If I could disarm him and get him out of the hotel room, Halle could make a run for it. Hopefully, someone saw him walking across the lot with an assault rifle and called the cops, if for no other reason than to back up Halle's story. But I didn't hear sirens yet.

One shot took out the locking mechanism. He kicked the door open and entered without checking behind it. Amateur.

I waited half a second then shoved the door with every ounce of strength I possessed. The rifle went flying, and I tackled him in his midsection, steering him outside. But he was big. He dug in and slowly pushed me back inside the room, my bare feet unable to get traction. We fell to the floor and rolled, each vying for the upper hand.

"Get 'im!" Aunt Lil shouted, shadowboxing as she looked on.

When he claimed the top position, I wedged a knee between us and dislodged him so I could scramble to my feet.

He stood, too. A little slower. A little stiffer. But he had bulk on his side. I had speed on mine.

He raised beefy fists, and I recognized the hand, the one holding a straight razor in the reflection of Halle's supposed suicide. The rage simmering beneath my boyish exterior began to boil the blood in my veins.

Why? Why would someone torment another human being for seventeen years? What did he get out of it besides a banal pleasure? Still, seventeen years. I couldn't wrap my head around it.

A humorous grin played about his bloodied mouth. "I was a boxer, too, sport." He'd looked into me. "And I wasn't hit by a truck yesterday."

I groaned. "Why does everyone keep saying that? I was sideswiped."

"Where is she?"

"You went to a lot of trouble to make Halle believe she'd killed you seventeen years ago."

"Yeah, well, she's worth it, don't you think?"

I ignored my knee-jerk reaction. "I do, actually."

"A little gullible, and her taste in men leaves a lot to be desired, but nobody's perfect."

"Is that the only way you can get a girl to notice you? Stalk her until she believes she's insane?"

He swung.

I ducked.

But he was faster than he looked. He caught my shoulder, and I fell back against the dresser. He rushed me while I was off balance, planning to use his weight to his advantage.

This would hurt.

After the truck incident, I was already sore. He had to weigh upwards of two hundred and fifty pounds. I calculated what that would do to my ribs and my chances of recovering enough to take him afterward. Then I thought about the beautiful woman in the bathtub. Of how frightened she must be. Odd how quickly the mind worked in these situations. Or maybe it was just my particular brain.

I hadn't taken a swing at an opponent in over five years. The last time I did, someone died, and my entire crew had paid the price by living on the run. But when I saw Meacham lunge forward, an instinct that had taken years of training to sharpen and hone flared, and I took the shot. A left hook to the jaw. One defensive blow. The exact same one that'd killed the guy at the bar all those years ago.

His head snapped to the side, and he crumpled, but inertia sent him flying into me. We crashed into the dresser, splintering the wood in two before we collapsed onto the floor.

I heard a hoot and a scream as Halle came running out, and Jason ran in. Aunt Lil hooted, but it was hard to tell which of the other two had screamed. I liked to think it was Jason.

Halle rushed over to me, grabbed my arm, and tried to pull me away from Meacham in a desperate attempt to save me, but he was out cold. I pulled her against me, lifted her chin until our eyes met, and chastised her. "You called Jason?" I asked, appalled. "I told you to call the cops."

"Jason's faster." She tried to squirm out of my grasp to check my wounds, but I held her steady. She felt good. And I was about to fall over. "And I did call the cops. They're on the way."

I looked at Jason. "Thanks for showing up too late to do any good, asshole."

He was still taking in the scene, as was Nolan, the hotel clerk who'd gone to high school with Halle and had probably had a crush on her ever since. "My boss is going to kill me. Is that a gun?"

"That was a nice shot, kid." Aunt Lil gave me two thumbs-up. "But did you know your hotel room is crawling with hellhounds?"

I glanced around. One by one, hellhounds melted out of the walls, stalking toward Meacham, their teeth bared as they emitted a low, guttural growl. They were massive, more like bears than hounds.

Meacham groaned and tried to get to his feet. He failed, ending up on his back, looking up at Halle and me. I wanted him to look forward to what his future held, but the only way to do that was to send him into limbo, a spiritual state between the living world and the dead.

I set Halle back, knelt beside him, and wrapped my hand around his throat. He was already halfway there. A little pressure for a few seconds should do the trick.

"Vause," Jason said.

"Vigil," I replied.

Halle knelt beside me. I expected her to try to stop me. Instead, she watched as I slowly drained the life out of his body, just enough for him to see them. For him to become aware.

When Meacham clawed at me, his thick jowls bulging out of his collar, his face turning a bright red, Jason walked over and put his foot on the guy's arm, holding it down much like I was his other one. "I can't condone this," my friend said, grinding his shoe into Meacham's wrist. "You're hurting him." He applied a bit more pressure, and Meacham cried out. "You have to stop." He could now say in a court of law that he tried to stop me, and I was oddly okay with him throwing me under the bus in that situation.

Meacham's eyes finally rolled back into his head, and he slowly became aware of the twelve massive beasts surrounding him. Some of them growled, drool dripping off their glistening teeth. Some barked and nipped at his feet and legs. Panic brought him back to consciousness, and I let go.

He choked and coughed, his gaze darting wildly about the room. "Wh–what was that?"

I, of course, looked while I had the chance. "When you die in your jail cell on December 3rd, 2033, at 2:08 in the morning of an apparent suicide, they'll be waiting. They'll rip your soul to shreds, wait for it to piece itself back together, then do it again. Over and over and over until hell opens up, and you get to meet your new master."

He gawked at me, the fear on his face palpable because he now knew. He now believed. Actions had consequences.

"And if you think it won't be painful, you're greatly, greatly mistaken."

Halle scooted closer to me, wrapping her arms around one of mine, wondering what I was talking about. I would have to explain later because she shouted so loudly, Jason jumped six inches. I may have, as well.

"Floraine!" she yelled, shoving out of my grasp and running out the door.

I wanted to go with her and make sure she was safe, but her only threat at the moment lay on the floor having a spiritual awakening.

Besides, I looked. The minute I saw her again, I looked and saw she would live a very long time.

* * * *

Two weeks later, Halle and I were saying our goodbyes to Jason and the gang. She was coming home with me to meet the fam, and we would decide where to go from there. I wanted her to be with her dad—who was thrilled with how things had turned out, despite needing a new head of security—and she wanted me to be with the juvenile delinquent destined to save the world. We were trying to come up with a compromise.

We stood by her truck, my bike on a trailer behind it, as I spoke with Jason. He wanted to talk to me before we left. Sounded important, so Halle took Flower for a walk to give us some alone time.

He gazed into the distance as though unable to look at me when he asked, "When and how?"

It took me a moment to realize he was asking about his fate. About his last moment. I'd wondered if I should tell him. Would it make any difference in the end? Would anything change?

I frowned and decided to give it a shot. "It's not something you want to know. Most fates are set in stone. Yours is no different."

He nodded, seemed to think for a moment, then repeated the question. "When and how?"

I stuck my hands into my pockets and said softly, "August, forty-three years from now. And violently." Jason had come into the world violently. He would leave it the same way, being the good Samaritan he was. Nothing I could say would change that.

He tsked and gave me a single shake of his head as he toed a rock at his feet. "Figures."

"Marry her."

"I plan to."

"And try to grow out of this asshole phase you're in."

"If you'll try to grow out of your bitch phase."

"Bitch?" I asked, only slightly offended.

"I forgot to tell you the other day, nice punch."

"Thanks. Is my haircut really that bad?"

"Not as bad as your face, but yeah."

"It's a delicate balance."

I watched Halle try to get Flower to shake with her. It *was* a delicate balance, as were most things in the universe.

* * * *

Also from 1001 Dark Nights and Darynda Jones, discover The Graveside Bar and Grill, The Graveyard Shift, The Gravedigger's Son.

Discover 1001 Dark Nights Collection Ten

DRAGON LOVER by Donna Grant
A Dragon Kings Novella

KEEPING YOU by Aurora Rose Reynolds
An Until Him/Her Novella

HAPPILY EVER NEVER by Carrie Ann Ryan
A Montgomery Ink Legacy Novella

DESTINED FOR ME by Corinne Michaels
A Come Back for Me/Say You'll Stay Crossover

MADAM ALANA by Audrey Carlan
A Marriage Auction Novella

DIRTY FILTHY BILLIONAIRE by Laurelin Paige
A Dirty Universe Novella

HIDE AND SEEK by Laura Kaye
A Blasphemy Novella

TANGLED WITH YOU by J. Kenner
A Stark Security Novella

TEMPTED by Lexi Blake
A Masters and Mercenaries Novella

THE DANDELION DIARY by Devney Perry
A Maysen Jar Novella

CHERRY LANE by Kristen Proby
A Huckleberry Bay Novella

THE GRAVE ROBBER by Darynda Jones
A Charley Davidson Novella

CRY OF THE BANSHEE by Heather Graham
A Krewe of Hunters Novella

DARKEST NEED by Rachel Van Dyken
A Dark Ones Novella

CHRISTMAS IN CAPE MAY by Jennifer Probst
A Sunshine Sisters Novella

A VAMPIRE'S MATE by Rebecca Zanetti
A Dark Protectors/Rebels Novella

WHERE IT BEGINS by Helena Hunting
A Pucked Novella

Also from Blue Box Press

THE MARRIAGE AUCTION by Audrey Carlan

THE JEWELER OF STOLEN DREAMS by M.J. Rose

SAPPHIRE STORM by Christopher Rice writing as C. Travis Rice
A Sapphire Cove Novel

ATLAS: THE STORY OF PA SALT by Lucinda Riley and Harry Whittaker

LOVE ON THE BYLINE by Xio Axelrod
A Plays and Players Novel

A SOUL OF ASH AND BLOOD by Jennifer L. Armentrout
A Blood and Ash Novel

START US UP by Lexi Blake
A Park Avenue Promise Novel

FIGHTING THE PULL by Kristen Ashley
A River Rain Novel

A FIRE IN THE FLESH by Jennifer L. Armentrout
A Flesh and Fire Novel

Discover More Darynda Jones

The Graveside Bar and Grill
A Charley Davidson Novella

When Donovan St. James' precocious charge asks him—no questions asked—to tail the doctor who keeps their ragtag team patched up, he wants to refuse. Not because the saucy teen is getting too big for her britches, ordering him around like a mob boss, but because the woman stirs feelings in him he would rather not explore. However, when evil threatens the doc's life, he realizes he has no choice. Sia saved his life once. He will try to return the favor. He just prays he can do it without losing his heart.

Running from the supernatural entity that has destroyed entire worlds to have her, Sia thought she'd found a haven on Earth with a motley team of warriors protecting the girl destined to save humanity. But when Sia's found, she realizes something on this plane is more scrumptious than her: that very teen. So, she runs—and Donovan St. James follows. Nothing is more alluring than a scruffy biker with a lacerating gaze. And she vows to tell him that…if they survive.

* * * *

The Gravedigger's Son
A Charley Davidson Novella

The job should have been easy.

Get in. Assess the situation. Get out. But for veteran tracker Quentin Rutherford, things get sticky when the girl he's loved since puberty shows up, conducting her own investigation into the strange occurrences of the small, New Mexico town. He knew it would be a risk coming back to the area, but he had no idea Amber Kowalski had become a bona fide PI, investigating things that go bump in the night. He shouldn't be surprised, however. She can see through the dead as clearly as he can. The real question is, can she see through him?

But is anything that's worth it ever easy?

To say that Amber is shocked to see her childhood crush would be the understatement of her fragile second life. One look at him tells her everything she needs to know. He's changed. So drastically she barely recognizes him. He is savage now, a hardened—in all the right places—demon hunter, and she is simply the awkward, lovestruck girl he left behind.

But she doesn't have time to dwell on the past. A supernatural entity has set up shop, and it's up to them to stop it before it kills again.

While thousands of questions burn inside her, she has to put her concern over him, over what he's become, aside for now. Because he's about to learn one, undeniable fact: she's changed, too.

* * * *

The Graveyard Shift
A Charley Davidson Novella

Guarding a precocious five-year-old who is half-human, half-god, and 100% destined to save the world is no easy feat.

Garrett Swopes was the ultimate skeptic until he met a certain hellion and her husband. They vanished after stopping a catastrophic event and left him, a mere mortal, in charge of protecting their gift to mankind. But when she disappears as well, he needs the help of another breed of hellion. One who can see past the veil of space and time. One who betrayed him.

She will get a truce in the deal, but she will never earn his forgiveness.

Marika Dubois's son—a warrior in the coming war between heaven and hell—was foreseen long before his birth. But to create a child strong enough to endure the trials that lay ahead, she needed a descendant of powerful magics. She found that in Garrett Swopes and tricked him into fathering her son. A ploy he has never forgiven her for. But when he knocks on her door asking for her help, she sees the fierce attraction he tries to deny rise within him.

And Marika has to decide if she dares risk her heart a second time to help the only man she's ever loved.

An excerpt from The Graveside Bar and Grill

A Charley Davidson Novella
By Darynda Jones
Now available!

Donovan froze. He held her against him until he could collect his thoughts. It took a while. After staring at her for a solid sixty seconds, he asked, "You're a what?" just to confirm.

Her huge eyes found his again, a stunning mixture of caramel and deeper browns with flecks of sea-foam green sprinkled throughout. "I mean, this body isn't, but I am. I've never... you know."

"Ah, got it." That made more sense. Not that a beautiful, successful woman couldn't be a virgin. The odds were definitely against it, though. "So, I'll be your first," he said matter-of-factly. No pressure.

"Technically. I mean, I know what to do. Technically. I've just never actually put that knowledge to the test."

"Is this a test?" he asked, grinning at her. She seemed more nervous than he was. "Tests were never my strong point in school."

"What was?"

"Girls, mostly."

She giggled. There was no other word for it. A short, soft bubble of laughter escaped her, and he found her even more enchanting because of it. "Why aren't I surprised?" she asked.

"I can't imagine. But first things first." He slipped the metal bracelet off, pushed the two ends together to close the circle, and slid it onto her much slenderer wrist. "It's still too big." He went to take it back but she snatched her hand away.

"It's perfect." She lifted it to study as though examining a cluster of diamonds. "But you really shouldn't have." When he only grinned at her, she added, "I feel like I'm leaving you vulnerable by taking this."

"He's not after me. I'll be fine."

She dropped her wrist and her gaze. "Should we start then?"

He lifted a brow. "Start?"

"Yeah, you know. It."

"Ah." He tried not to smile. He failed. This was going to be fun. "Where do you suggest we begin?"

"Oh." Her eyes rounded as she thought about his question much more intently than he'd imagined she would. "Right. Well, music seems to be important."

"Music." He nodded and fought that errant grin again. The fucker. "What would you suggest?"

"I'm not sure." She pressed her mouth to one side as she considered it. "Maybe something bow-chicka-wow-ish?"

He had to refocus every ounce of strength in his body to keep from laughing. To hide his face, he leaned past her to turn on the radio. "Let's just see what's available."

"Right. Good idea."

After a quick search, something appropriately smooth came on.

"Oh, Rihanna!" she said, clapping softly. Then, as though embarrassed, she added, "This is a good song."

"I'll take your word for it. What next?"

"Hmmm." She tapped her chin with an index finger. "Well, I don't want to seem forward—"

"Of course, not."

"—but you should probably take off your shirt."

"Just me?"

She glanced down at her zippered hoodie. "Good point. I mean, it's only fair, right?"

"Fair is fair."

"Fair is definitely fair." She started to unzip the hoodie but stopped when he didn't move to do the same.

When she pointed her chin at the T-shirt, he reached for the back of the collar and lifted it over his head. He could've sworn he heard a soft gasp, but he wasn't sure.

He tossed Swopes' tee onto the passenger's seat, and she slowly lowered the zipper on her hoodie without taking her eyes off his chest. He suddenly worried that his tattoos would turn her off. She didn't seem to be bothered, but there was an entire demographic that found them appalling. Which was probably a big part of the reason he'd gotten them in the first place. Nothing like presenting himself as a hellraiser to keep the puritans at bay. He was a walking defense mechanism. Would she see through him? Did he care?

With a jolt of surprise, he realized that he did. But why? He'd never cared. Then again, he'd never met anyone like the doc. And that was before he knew what she was. Most of the women he'd taken to his bed had practically begged him to do so. He'd never hit on a woman in his life. He'd never had to. But the doc was different. He could see himself begging for her attention. Willingly. Gladly. Desperately.

When she literally separated one tooth of the zipper at a time, her movements painstakingly slow, he couldn't take it any longer. He took the zipper out of her hands, slid it all the way down, and peeled the jacket off her shoulders.

Her powerful scent engulfed him. Exotic and sweet, it surrounded, saturated, and stirred, pumping blood into his cock. When she started on the buttons of her white blouse, he didn't have it in him to wait. Praying the garment didn't cost more than his Harley, he took the edges and ripped it open. Her breasts, held by the barest hint of a lace bra, spilled forth, and for a moment, he was mesmerized. Until his gaze dropped to her stomach. To the side of her ribs. To her right shoulder.

It was like someone threw a bucket of ice water on him. No, not ice water. Boiling honey. When she went to cover her midsection with her arms, he didn't let her. He took hold of her wrists and locked them behind her back for a better look.

Scars of every size and shape adorned her beautiful body, and his blood turned bitingly cold. He didn't realize how much so until she winced and jerked her hands out of his grip.

"I'm sorry," he said, but it was too late. He'd ruined the mood. He bit back a curse when she pulled her shirt together and climbed off his lap.

About Darynda Jones

NY Times and *USA Today* Bestselling Author Darynda Jones has won numerous awards for her work and her books have been translated into 17 languages. As a born storyteller, Darynda grew up spinning tales of dashing damsels and heroes in distress for any unfortunate soul who happened by, certain they went away the better for it. She penned the internationally bestselling Charley Davidson series and is currently working on several beloved projects, most notably the Sunshine Vicram Mystery Series with St. Martin's Press and the Betwixt and Between Series of paranormal women's fiction. She lives in the Land of Enchantment, also known as New Mexico, with her husband and two beautiful sons, the Mighty, Mighty Jones Boys.

She can be found at http://www.daryndajones.com

Discover 1001 Dark Nights

COLLECTION ONE
FOREVER WICKED by Shayla Black ~ CRIMSON TWILIGHT by Heather Graham ~ CAPTURED IN SURRENDER by Liliana Hart ~ SILENT BITE: A SCANGUARDS WEDDING by Tina Folsom ~ DUNGEON GAMES by Lexi Blake ~ AZAGOTH by Larissa Ione ~ NEED YOU NOW by Lisa Renee Jones ~ SHOW ME, BABY by Cherise Sinclair~ ROPED IN by Lorelei James ~ TEMPTED BY MIDNIGHT by Lara Adrian ~ THE FLAME by Christopher Rice ~ CARESS OF DARKNESS by Julie Kenner

COLLECTION TWO
WICKED WOLF by Carrie Ann Ryan ~ WHEN IRISH EYES ARE HAUNTING by Heather Graham ~ EASY WITH YOU by Kristen Proby ~ MASTER OF FREEDOM by Cherise Sinclair ~ CARESS OF PLEASURE by Julie Kenner ~ ADORED by Lexi Blake ~ HADES by Larissa Ione ~ RAVAGED by Elisabeth Naughton ~ DREAM OF YOU by Jennifer L. Armentrout ~ STRIPPED DOWN by Lorelei James ~ RAGE/KILLIAN by Alexandra Ivy/Laura Wright ~ DRAGON KING by Donna Grant ~ PURE WICKED by Shayla Black ~ HARD AS STEEL by Laura Kaye ~ STROKE OF MIDNIGHT by Lara Adrian ~ ALL HALLOWS EVE by Heather Graham ~ KISS THE FLAME by Christopher Rice~ DARING HER LOVE by Melissa Foster ~ TEASED by Rebecca Zanetti ~ THE PROMISE OF SURRENDER by Liliana Hart

COLLECTION THREE
HIDDEN INK by Carrie Ann Ryan ~ BLOOD ON THE BAYOU by Heather Graham ~ SEARCHING FOR MINE by Jennifer Probst ~ DANCE OF DESIRE by Christopher Rice ~ ROUGH RHYTHM by Tessa Bailey ~ DEVOTED by Lexi Blake ~ Z by Larissa Ione ~ FALLING UNDER YOU by Laurelin Paige ~ EASY FOR KEEPS by Kristen Proby ~ UNCHAINED by Elisabeth Naughton ~ HARD TO SERVE by Laura Kaye ~ DRAGON FEVER by Donna Grant ~ KAYDEN/SIMON by Alexandra Ivy/Laura Wright ~ STRUNG UP by Lorelei James ~ MIDNIGHT UNTAMED by Lara Adrian ~ TRICKED by Rebecca Zanetti ~ DIRTY WICKED by Shayla Black ~ THE ONLY ONE by Lauren Blakely ~ SWEET SURRENDER by Liliana Hart

COLLECTION FOUR

ROCK CHICK REAWAKENING by Kristen Ashley ~ ADORING INK by Carrie Ann Ryan ~ SWEET RIVALRY by K. Bromberg ~ SHADE'S LADY by Joanna Wylde ~ RAZR by Larissa Ione ~ ARRANGED by Lexi Blake ~ TANGLED by Rebecca Zanetti ~ HOLD ME by J. Kenner ~ SOMEHOW, SOME WAY by Jennifer Probst ~ TOO CLOSE TO CALL by Tessa Bailey ~ HUNTED by Elisabeth Naughton ~ EYES ON YOU by Laura Kaye ~ BLADE by Alexandra Ivy/Laura Wright ~ DRAGON BURN by Donna Grant ~ TRIPPED OUT by Lorelei James ~ STUD FINDER by Lauren Blakely ~ MIDNIGHT UNLEASHED by Lara Adrian ~ HALLOW BE THE HAUNT by Heather Graham ~ DIRTY FILTHY FIX by Laurelin Paige ~ THE BED MATE by Kendall Ryan ~ NIGHT GAMES by CD Reiss ~ NO RESERVATIONS by Kristen Proby ~ DAWN OF SURRENDER by Liliana Hart

COLLECTION FIVE

BLAZE ERUPTING by Rebecca Zanetti ~ ROUGH RIDE by Kristen Ashley ~ HAWKYN by Larissa Ione ~ RIDE DIRTY by Laura Kaye ~ ROME'S CHANCE by Joanna Wylde ~ THE MARRIAGE ARRANGEMENT by Jennifer Probst ~ SURRENDER by Elisabeth Naughton ~ INKED NIGHTS by Carrie Ann Ryan ~ ENVY by Rachel Van Dyken ~ PROTECTED by Lexi Blake ~ THE PRINCE by Jennifer L. Armentrout ~ PLEASE ME by J. Kenner ~ WOUND TIGHT by Lorelei James ~ STRONG by Kylie Scott ~ DRAGON NIGHT by Donna Grant ~ TEMPTING BROOKE by Kristen Proby ~ HAUNTED BE THE HOLIDAYS by Heather Graham ~ CONTROL by K. Bromberg ~ HUNKY HEARTBREAKER by Kendall Ryan ~ THE DARKEST CAPTIVE by Gena Showalter

COLLECTION SIX

DRAGON CLAIMED by Donna Grant ~ ASHES TO INK by Carrie Ann Ryan ~ ENSNARED by Elisabeth Naughton ~ EVERMORE by Corinne Michaels ~ VENGEANCE by Rebecca Zanetti ~ ELI'S TRIUMPH by Joanna Wylde ~ CIPHER by Larissa Ione ~ RESCUING MACIE by Susan Stoker ~ ENCHANTED by Lexi Blake ~ TAKE THE BRIDE by Carly Phillips ~ INDULGE ME by J. Kenner ~ THE KING by Jennifer L. Armentrout ~ QUIET MAN by Kristen Ashley ~ ABANDON by Rachel Van Dyken ~ THE OPEN DOOR by Laurelin Paige ~ CLOSER by Kylie Scott ~ SOMETHING JUST LIKE THIS by

Jennifer Probst ~ BLOOD NIGHT by Heather Graham ~ TWIST OF FATE by Jill Shalvis ~ MORE THAN PLEASURE YOU by Shayla Black ~ WONDER WITH ME by Kristen Proby ~ THE DARKEST ASSASSIN by Gena Showalter

COLLECTION SEVEN

THE BISHOP by Skye Warren ~ TAKEN WITH YOU by Carrie Ann Ryan ~ DRAGON LOST by Donna Grant ~ SEXY LOVE by Carly Phillips ~ PROVOKE by Rachel Van Dyken ~ RAFE by Sawyer Bennett ~ THE NAUGHTY PRINCESS by Claire Contreras ~ THE GRAVEYARD SHIFT by Darynda Jones ~ CHARMED by Lexi Blake ~ SACRIFICE OF DARKNESS by Alexandra Ivy ~ THE QUEEN by Jen Armentrout ~ BEGIN AGAIN by Jennifer Probst ~ VIXEN by Rebecca Zanetti ~ SLASH by Laurelin Paige ~ THE DEAD HEAT OF SUMMER by Heather Graham ~ WILD FIRE by Kristen Ashley ~ MORE THAN PROTECT YOU by Shayla Black ~ LOVE SONG by Kylie Scott ~ CHERISH ME by J. Kenner ~ SHINE WITH ME by Kristen Proby

COLLECTION EIGHT

DRAGON REVEALED by Donna Grant ~ CAPTURED IN INK by Carrie Ann Ryan ~ SECURING JANE by Susan Stoker ~ WILD WIND by Kristen Ashley ~ DARE TO TEASE by Carly Phillips ~ VAMPIRE by Rebecca Zanetti ~ MAFIA KING by Rachel Van Dyken ~ THE GRAVEDIGGER'S SON by Darynda Jones ~ FINALE by Skye Warren ~ MEMORIES OF YOU by J. Kenner ~ SLAYED BY DARKNESS by Alexandra Ivy ~ TREASURED by Lexi Blake ~ THE DAREDEVIL by Dylan Allen ~ BOND OF DESTINY by Larissa Ione ~ MORE THAN POSSESS YOU by Shayla Black ~ HAUNTED HOUSE by Heather Graham ~ MAN FOR ME by Laurelin Paige ~ THE RHYTHM METHOD by Kylie Scott ~ JONAH BENNETT by Tijan ~ CHANGE WITH ME by Kristen Proby ~ THE DARKEST DESTINY by Gena Showalter

COLLECTION NINE

DRAGON UNBOUND by Donna Grant ~ NOTHING BUT INK by Carrie Ann Ryan ~ THE MASTERMIND by Dylan Allen ~ JUST ONE WISH by Carly Phillips ~ BEHIND CLOSED DOORS by Skye Warren ~ GOSSAMER IN THE DARKNESS by Kristen Ashley ~ THE CLOSE-UP by Kennedy Ryan ~ DELIGHTED by Lexi Blake ~ THE

GRAVESIDE BAR AND GRILL by Darynda Jones ~ THE ANTI-FAN AND THE IDOL by Rachel Van Dyken ~ CHARMED BY YOU by J. Kenner ~ DESCEND TO DARKNESS by Heather Graham~ BOND OF PASSION by Larissa Ione ~ JUST WHAT I NEEDED by Kylie Scott

Discover Blue Box Press

TAME ME by J. Kenner ~ TEMPT ME by J. Kenner ~ DAMIEN by J. Kenner ~ TEASE ME by J. Kenner ~ REAPER by Larissa Ione ~ THE SURRENDER GATE by Christopher Rice ~ SERVICING THE TARGET by Cherise Sinclair ~ THE LAKE OF LEARNING by Steve Berry and M.J. Rose ~ THE MUSEUM OF MYSTERIES by Steve Berry and M.J. Rose ~ TEASE ME by J. Kenner ~ FROM BLOOD AND ASH by Jennifer L. Armentrout ~ QUEEN MOVE by Kennedy Ryan ~ THE HOUSE OF LONG AGO by Steve Berry and M.J. Rose ~ THE BUTTERFLY ROOM by Lucinda Riley ~ A KINGDOM OF FLESH AND FIRE by Jennifer L. Armentrout ~ THE LAST TIARA by M.J. Rose ~ THE CROWN OF GILDED BONES by Jennifer L. Armentrout ~ THE MISSING SISTER by Lucinda Riley ~ THE END OF FOREVER by Steve Berry and M.J. Rose ~ THE STEAL by C. W. Gortner and M.J. Rose ~ CHASING SERENITY by Kristen Ashley ~ A SHADOW IN THE EMBER by Jennifer L. Armentrout ~ THE BAIT by C.W. Gortner and M.J. Rose ~ THE FASHION ORPHANS by Randy Susan Meyers and M.J. Rose ~ TAKING THE LEAP by Kristen Ashley ~ SAPPHIRE SUNSET by Christopher Rice writing C. Travis Rice ~ THE WAR OF TWO QUEENS by Jennifer L. Armentrout ~ THE MURDERS AT FLEAT HOUSE by Lucinda Riley ~ THE HEIST by C.W. Gortner and M.J. Rose ~ SAPPHIRE SPRING by Christopher Rice writing as C. Travis Rice ~ MAKING THE MATCH by Kristen Ashley ~ A LIGHT IN THE FLAME by Jennifer L.

On Behalf of 1001 Dark Nights,

Liz Berry, M.J. Rose, and Jillian Stein would like to thank ~

Steve Berry
Doug Scofield
Benjamin Stein
Kim Guidroz
Chelle Olson
Tanaka Kangara
Asha Hossain
Chris Graham
Jessica Saunders
Stacey Tardif
Dylan Stockton
Kate Boggs
Richard Blake
and Simon Lipskar

Made in United States
Troutdale, OR
09/15/2023

12914372R00072